TURKEY TRACKS

Lizbie Brown

St. Martin's Press
New York

Also by Lizbie Brown

Golden Dolly (Pageant Books, USA, 1988)
Broken Star (St. Martin's Press, 1993)

Library of Congress Cataloging-in-Publication Data

Brown, Lizbie.
Turkey tracks / Lizbie Brown.
p.   cm.
ISBN 0-312-13193-3 (hardcover)
I. Title.
PR6052.R6136T87   1995
813'.54—dc20   95-1733   CIP

First published in Great Britain by
Constable & Company Ltd.

First U.S. Edition: June 1995
10   9   8   7   6   5   4   3   2   1

1

There had been no premonition that this Monday was to be different from any other. When the telephone rang, Elizabeth picked it up at once.

'Hello? Is that the patchwork shop in Pierrepont Mews?'

'It is.'

'I wish to speak to the proprietor, Elizabeth Blair.'

'Speaking.'

'Margaret Fleming here. Publicity director for the Wetherburn Museum. I trust you've heard of us?'

'Indeed I have!'

'I wondered if I might ask a small favour?'

'Ask away.'

'This is a trifle difficult. You may or may not have heard that we have . . . well, a crisis on our hands.'

'I heard they cut your Museum Council grant.'

'Well, that's not quite what I was referring to. Look – there's no way I can approach this with delicacy . . .'

Elizabeth waited.

'The fact is, something rather horrific happened here last night. We had an intruder. Joanna Drew, the curator's sister, was attacked. Shot dead . . .'

'Good golly!'

'Yes, well . . . Naturally, we're all shocked. Which brings me to the reason for this call. We've been running a series of lectures on the History of Patchwork.'

'I'm aware of that. Saw your poster in the library.'

'The thing is, our lecturer, Jane Maddocks, feels too upset by her sister-in-law's death to carry on, so we're seeking a temporary replacement. And your name came up.'

'Really?'

'The next lecture's due on Wednesday afternoon.'

'With respect, I'm amazed you're even thinking of holding it.'

'We did consider postponing, but Tom – Mr Maddocks – says Joanna would want it to go on. And the police haven't raised any real objections, our lecture room being well away from the scene of the crime.'

'Forgive me. I'd like to help, but –'

'It would only be for a week or two.'

'I really don't think –'

'Take your time. You don't have to make a decision now. I can ring you back.'

'Look, I'm afraid –'

'Believe me, I understand that you're a very busy lady. And you may not wish to take on a course that's half-way through. But I must just emphasize that you could pick up a lot of valuable orders from our ladies. Let's face it, we've all been affected by this dreadful recession . . .'

'Well . . .'

'And with Christmas approaching . . .'

'I suppose I might just manage a couple of weeks . . .'

'That would do for a start. Could you get up here this afternoon so that I can show you the ropes?'

'Today's difficult.'

'Shall we say two-ish? I won't keep you long.'

'I really can't make today. What time is your lecture scheduled on Wednesday?'

'Two thirty. But –'

'I'll come up at one. There'll be time for a chat before I launch myself on your ladies.'

'That'll have to do, then. I'll have the file with Jane's lecture notes sent down to you.'

'No, I'll do my own thing, if that's OK with you.'

'I think Mrs Maddocks would prefer you to stick to the set course.'

'I'm sure she would, but if you want me to do the job . . .'

'Very well. As you wish . . .'

'Max. It's Elizabeth.'

'Betsy! The old varicose veins playing up? You can't climb the stairs any more?'

'Caroline's off sick. I can't leave the shop. Did you hear about this murder up at the Wetherburn?'

'Yeah. It was on Radio Bristol.'

'I've just had a call from their pushy publicity lady.'

'I hope you told her she's doing a good job?'

'She ran rings around me. She wants me to . . . Good lord!'

'Elizabeth . . .? You still there?'

'Yes. I'm sorry. But take a look out of the window.'

'Hold on.'

'Well? Do you see what I see?'

'I'm afraid so. So how much did you pay him . . . her? It?'

'I didn't pay anybody. It's nothing to do with me, Max.'

'Come off it! You do come from a little ole place called Turkey Creek.'

'And it's Thanksgiving. Well, almost. But I still don't hire jerks in turkey costumes to stand outside my shop. What's that infernal din down by the Abbey? Can you hear it? Open the window.'

'Can't. It's stuck. Sounds like one of those vans with a loud-speaker. Local elections, maybe. So what did the Wetherburn woman want?'

'I'll tell you over coffee. I've just brewed.'

'Give me two minutes. I've got a phone call to make. A new client.'

'Yes?'

'Mrs Weston? Helen? Max Shepard here.'

'Oh, hello.'

'Listen, I was wondering if I could drop in on you later. I need more information about your husband. The more I know about him, the quicker we'll find your children. Would four o'clock suit you?'

'What? Oh . . . yes. That's fine.'

'And if you could jot down in the meantime anything . . . anything at all that might give me a lead . . . Hello? Are you still there?'

'Yes. I'm here. I'm sorry. I took a sleeping pill. They make you . . . hazy . . .'

'Let me just check your address.'

'It's 15, Henry Road.'

'Where is that?'

'Off the London Road. Turn left at the traffic lights. It's a terraced cottage. Flaky yellow front door . . .'

'Right. I'll see you at four.'

When Max came thumping down the staircase from his office on the first floor, the turkey was still standing outside Elizabeth's shop window. Six foot tall, with black felt legs and a scraggy comb. Its eyes were blank and still, as though its spirit had gone away and left its long, daft body standing there, mesmerized by the colours of the quilts on this grey November afternoon.

Max eyed the scarlet paint splashed over its flanks. 'Splendidly tacky,' he said. 'What's he advertising?'

Elizabeth said, 'Haven't a clue, but I've seen better birds. Shut the door. There's a draught.'

It was a bitingly cold day, with an east wind that was storming through the alleys as if it had been cooped up all night and had just been let out. But the shop called Martha Washington was gently warm from the gas fire in the restored Victorian grate and the collection of quilts in the window acted as a comforter against the bleaker world outside. The old Durham pink and white strippy that Elizabeth had snatched from a rummage sale. The particularly swell Log Cabin in all the pastels from blue to clover and back again. But most of all, the serenely pieced red and oak-leaf green Turkey Tracks that her son, Jim Junior, had sent over from Virginia only a week or so ago. The Turkey Tracks with its fifteen-inch blocks and straight furrow quilting was the one that turned passers-by cod-eyed, made their fingers fidget so that they just had to come in and touch it.

Whether they bought or not was another thing these days, as that blasted Fleming woman had been so quick to point out.

The business had had an indifferent summer, followed by an

uninspiring fall. Not that Elizabeth had expected to make a pile when she crossed the Atlantic – two years ago now – to live in the West of England. It was her passion for the honey-coloured Regency terraces of Bath that had persuaded her to launch Martha Washington.

Originally, she had come over on vacation to get over the death of her husband (and to research her West Country ancestors), but she had fallen for the city, hook, line and sinker. Though her dismayed family was constantly nagging at her to come on home where she belonged, she had no intention – well not yet, at least – of complying with their wishes. She felt comfortable in her doll's house of a shop in Pierrepont Mews (and in her cottage in the nearby village of South Harptree). Had grown accustomed to the diversions provided by her young friend Max's detective agency upstairs on the first floor.

So there it was. So long as you made a bit to live on and didn't get into *too* intense a relationship with your bank manager . . . Passion of that kind was for kids of Max's age.

Well, in theory. The fact was that these days, anyone – even the comparatively well-heeled – could find himself in financial trouble. When you switched on the TV at night, you thought, God, not again, thousands more losing their jobs and their independence. Sound people of mature years out on their ear and oscillating between anger and despair. Whole roomfuls of quilts wouldn't settle them down in this dark economic night . . .

The turkey seemed to be shivering. It shuffled forward, so as to bring itself nearer the warmth of the window.

'He's cold,' said Elizabeth. 'Should I ask him in for a cuppa?'

Max's intensely blue gaze rested on the bird. 'I wouldn't bother.'

'Why not? He looks friendly.'

'So did the Trojan horse.'

Down by the Guildhall, the loudspeaker was still blasting out bursts of static to be scattered on the wind first in one direction, then the other. It was like trying to listen to a British Rail announcement. Impeccable diction, pity about the spurt and crackle that made it impossible to catch a single word.

Elizabeth eyed Max over the top of her half-moon spectacles. 'I could do with the publicity. You could pop up and get your camera.'

'You wouldn't like that kind of publicity,' Max said, looking as if a door had just opened in his brain. The turkey was scrabbling for something in the leather pouch around its neck. The fuzz in the distance grew clearer. The odd phrase began to emerge from the aural fog. *'Murderers! Hot blades . . .'*

'Why not? He may as well boost my establishment as Miss Millie's or the Kentucky Fried.'

'Miss Millie's be damned!' Max flipped a hand through his thick brown hair. 'Don't you remember? They fire-bombed a couple of farms near Trowbridge.'

'Giant turkeys?' Elizabeth wondered which of them was going mad.

'The Animal Liberation Front. Pre-Christmas campaign. I've got a file on them as long as your arm. As a matter of fact, some chap near you – local farmer . . . Reuben Dando – just called me to investigate the attacks on his farm.'

'Tithebarn . . . They set fire to his vans and his Range Rover.' She still couldn't connect this dopey-looking bird with urban terrorism.

'That's it. Commando-style raids. They got clean away. Slippery customers, the ALF.'

Suddenly, the turkey moved. Plastered something hard against the window.

'Hey!' Elizabeth took a step towards the door.

'Funny thing is, Reuben was up at the Wetherburn nearly every night last week, patrolling the grounds. He's an old friend of the Maddockses'. Apparently they've had problems with the ALF too. And the only night nobody checked the place, Mrs Drew was murdered.'

He was wasting his breath. Elizabeth was no longer there. Her matronly-but-trim form had nipped out through the door to peel off the poster that their feathered friend had stuck to the glass.

Now his ungainly legs were plodding off down the mews.

They didn't mean you to miss anything, the ALF. Their missive was printed in scarlet capitals, as large as a barn, on recycled paper. She held it at arm's length to read it:

SUPPORT TURKEYS' LIB
STOP THE SHAMEFUL SLAUGHTER
HOW WOULD YOU LIKE TO SPEND YOUR LIFE IN A CAGE TWELVE
INCHES BY TEN? NEVER TO SEE DAYLIGHT UNTIL TAKEN OUT TO BE

KILLED? NEVER TO BREATHE AIR UNTAINTED WITH AMMONIA FROM YOUR OWN DROPPINGS? THINK ABOUT IT, THEN SEE HOW YOU ENJOY YOUR CHICKEN SANDWICH. SHUT THESE BLOODY BELSENS IN THE NAME OF HUMANITY!

Elizabeth passed it to Max and went with a poker face to pour the coffee in the small back room. She should never have read the thing. Now she would feel guilty, get squeamish every time she ate chicken pot pie. She remembered suddenly all sorts of village gossip about what went on up at Reuben Dando's factory farm. Who was it that had told her about the vast rows of battery cages? About the time there had been a mechanical failure in the ventilation and thousands of birds had suffocated? Must have been Dottie Marchant, next door. Yes, Dottie had called it a sin against life. But the locals turned a blind eye to such practices because Reuben employed them. And his family had been up at Tithebarn for almost a century; he was a churchwarden, a parish councillor and a cornerstone of South Harptree village life . . .

'Maybe I'll turn veggy,' said Max when she handed him his coffee.

'And pigs might fly,' said Elizabeth, getting out the shortbread fingers. Max's idealistic notions were here today and gone tomorrow.

'Helen's a vegetarian.'

'Who's Helen?'

'My newest client. She came rushing in last night just before I shut up shop. She wants me to trace her two children. Her ex-husband snatched them from school the other night. Invented a dental appointment and picked them up before she got there. I'd put down sods like that,' he said. His voice sounded grim for once, almost menacing.

'He must love them,' Elizabeth said, 'or he wouldn't have done it. Not that I'm excusing him.'

'She says he didn't do it out of love. Just jealousy.' Max's biscuit paused, half-way to his mouth. 'She's worried that he'll harm them. Apparently, he's handy with his fists when he's had a few.'

'One of those.' The light from the lamp caught the silver flecks in her tawny-to-blonde hair.

'Yes.'

'Not so good.'

11

'Exactly. I know I'm stupid, but why do women like her fall for fruitcakes like that? I mean, she's a real stunner, Elizabeth. The kind of woman who makes you dance inside . . .'

It was clear from the expression in his eyes that one of Max's whirlwind passions was at ignition point and launching. She no longer bothered to try and bring him back down to earth, merely marvelled at the power of his lift-off and how much fuel there was in the tank.

She said, 'I guess sometimes you don't check people's baggage until it's too late.'

He wasn't listening. 'There's something about her eyes. They're sort of amber-coloured . . . you know? You can see she'd be serene if life hadn't done this to her.'

'There's always one fly in the honey pot, Max. You gonna drink that coffee or let it go cold?'

There was no reply. I'd get more sense out of that damned turkey, she thought. Then wondered, uneasily, why her shop had been singled out for such close attention.

2

'Access to the Exhibition Centre only, madam. Are you one of the lecture ladies?' The young policeman stood with his shoulders shrugged up against the cold. Clearly he hadn't had lunch and was waiting for someone to take his place at the gate, so that he could go and stuff his thin, young face with crispy bacon sandwiches and hot tea.

'I'm *the* lecture lady,' Elizabeth told him. 'And I have an appointment with Mrs Fleming in the main house.'

'I'll have to check that, if you don't mind waiting.'

She closed the window again. It was as cold as charity. White mist enveloped the Wetherburn, cutting off the mansion from the chequerboard of fields and winter woods in the valley below. There was that lurking sense of stillness that came with November fog and yew hedges thick with frost and sunlight so thin that it was almost transparent.

It was just as cold back home. Last night she had picked up the receiver and dialled her brother's number. 'Hal? Is that you?'

'Elizabeth?'

'Yes, it's me. Did Hannah go?'

'Last Saturday.'

'And did you hear from her?'

'Oh, sure. She's sitting down there in Louisiana in the sun under a banana tree. Twenty-five years together and she goes off on a six-months sabbatical without a backward look. Makes you think, doesn't it?'

'She thinks the change will do you good.'

'You're not kidding! She said I was getting to look like Bozo and it would do me good to be pitched out of my rut.'

Bozo was Hal's dog. A hairy old mutt much given to mooching around the golf course and hogging the most comfortable corner of the sofa. Come to think of it, Hannah had a point.

'I might go out and seduce one of my students. Whaddya think?'

'Right this minute?'

'Well, tomorrow.'

'You need a good dinner inside you?'

There was a lugubrious grunt.

'And time to work out tactics.'

'How are the mighty fallen . . . ' she said, laughing.

Hal had been dazzling when young. But weren't we all? Elizabeth thought. The policeman was waiting for his radio to talk back at him. A serious young man with a serious young moustache. Behind him, a pair of winter birds sat huddled on a bare branch.

Yes, Hal could have had any girl he wanted. He was her favourite brother, the one who had taught her to swim and climb trees and catch a football. Had taught her to drive, too, in the old station wagon with the dark leather interior. She could see him now in his checked woollen shirt, standing by the satin-smooth wooden banisters in the big house with the barn attached.

'I don't suppose you'll be back for Thanksgiving?'

Thanksgiving . . . Pumpkin pie and cornbread, candied sweet potatoes and blueberries from a mountain farm. 'Sorry, honey,' she said regretfully. 'Can't leave the shop. You come over and visit me. Cheer yourself up.'

'To England?'

13

He sounded comically startled.

'That's where I am, Hal.'

'Well, now, I don't think so.'

'Why not?'

'Oh . . . I like a decent turkey.'

'I think we could provide you with that,' she said, remembering the apparition in the mews.

'I doubt it. I've heard about English food.'

'Oh, come on, you old grouch! Catch a plane. Get over here!'

The policeman packed away his walkie-talkie and waved her on in through the double wrought-iron gates. Beyond the covered wagon and the Indian tepee (the Wetherburn specialized in Americana) to the right of the main house, two WPCs were measuring distances. A newish building to the left of the main house was screened off by yellow plastic ribbons, lurid against the frosted lawns surrounding the Colonial Herb Garden.

She parked the Citroën under the trees in the empty car-park. Went down the winding steps to the gravelled drive. The immensely tall mansion – Regency – gazed serenely out over the valley. Beechwoods encircled the terraces that ran down to a small lake which, in summer, was used for boating. It was very quiet and smelled of nothing more sinister than grass and parkland. A pair of huge stone urns guarded the main entrance.

Elizabeth pushed open one of the twin doors. The main hall was empty except for a long, mahogany table that held information leaflets and guidebooks and an indifferent bunch of dried flowers in a slipware jug. Eighteenth-century windows did their best to let in the monotonous wintry light, illuminating the giant Confederate flag that hung over the staircase and the case containing the bullets that killed Stonewall Jackson at Chancellorsville. Perhaps it was the weather, but she caught an almost tangible whiff of time and decay. The rooms, devoid of visitors, were flat and shadowy behind drawn blinds; a fine gloom the colour of alabaster stole into every corner.

'Mrs Blair? This way. Margaret says to come up.'

The woman calling down from the curve of the staircase was square-built, with a no-nonsense Yorkshire accent. Her clothes were of the decent rummage sale variety. Baggy brown cardy and lace-up brogues of the kind used for earthing in dahlia tubers.

'You made me jump. I didn't see you up there.'

'Heard the door bang. Drives you mad after a while. Still, as I was just saying to Margaret, it's the silent callers you have to worry about.'

'Like your intruder the other night? Such a shock for you all!'

'Well, the newspapers and the television's full of such horrors. You just don't expect it to happen in your own back garden. I'm Madge Radley, by the way. I work here three days a week as a guide.'

They didn't hang around in Yorkshire, legs like steam pistons. Elizabeth could scarcely keep up.

'The police have been swarming around for days . . . The Chief Constable and the Detective Chief Super and the Chief Chief Super. They drink tea by the gallon. Helps the jolly old grey cells, one must presume.'

'So do you enjoy working as a guide?'

'Yes, I do, though I could never have imagined myself doing such a thing. I started coming up here with the St John's Ambulance when they had their fêtes . . . oh, yonks ago. And I sort of fell for the place, you know? It grows on you. Then one of the regular guides fell ill and I took her place for a while. You might say, I got sucked into the place. Well, here we are. Margaret's is the outer office and her husband, Oliver, who balances the books, works in the inner sanctum. I'll buzz back later to take you across to the lecture room.'

Elizabeth was shown into a long, tall room with a double row of bookshelves. Margaret Fleming sat signing letters behind a meticulously ordered desk. She stood up to shake hands. 'Mrs Blair! How nice to meet you! Have a chair. It really is so kind of you to help us out.'

She was fifty, perhaps, with carefully preserved brown hair and a face that was all angles and sharp edges. Her smile was welcoming, but very possibly that was ill temper lurking behind it.

The room had once been twice the size, Elizabeth decided. The wreathed plasterwork on the ceiling had been cut in half abruptly above the cheaply varnished inner door. There was something mean-spirited about chopping up an elegant room like that. Ramming a thin partition across it and cramming too much mahogany furniture around the long windows.

So what was on the other side of the inner door? Margaret Fleming's better half, presumably.

The stone fireplace would have heated half the second storey had there been anything laid in it. Margaret Fleming caught Elizabeth looking at it.

'Are you cold? We keep the heating turned down, I'm afraid, when we're not open to the public. It saves a fortune in bills and helps preserve the exhibits.'

'I can imagine. No, I'm not cold,' Elizabeth lied.

'May I take your coat, then?'

'I'll keep it on, thanks.'

The park outside lay shrouded in a silvery mist that was bluer up by the woods than in the gardens below. The low-hanging boughs of the old lime trees formed a frosted curtain that served as a backdrop to the opposite wing of the house. Two rows of windows faced each other, like watching eyes, across the central courtyard. It would be like working in a goldfish bowl, Elizabeth thought. One half of the building always knowing what the other half was doing.

She brought out her dry smile. 'I had one hell of a job getting in here! Police all over the place. Must be difficult for you.'

'Bizarre!' Mrs Fleming shuddered. 'But then, it's all been so weird that I still can't believe it happened. Joanna lying dead in the middle of all that circus stuff . . .'

Elizabeth had devoured all the details in the newspapers. The corpse had been found lying in the Exhibition Centre amid the wreckage of a hand-carved, five-hundred-foot circus parade, with carousel horses and assorted Indian carvings, that was on loan from the Shelburne Museum in Vermont.

Quite a send-off, she thought. 'I gather you were setting up an exhibition of folk art?'

Margaret Fleming kept squaring up the pen to the jotter. 'Yes. Tom . . . Mr Maddocks . . . has family connections in the States. That's very useful to us. His mother was American.' She picked up the phone and said in a clipped voice, 'Anne – we'll have the tea now. And don't forget the gingerbread.'

'And this house was originally the Maddocks family home?'

'Still is. Tom and Jane have a large flat at the back of the house.'

'And Mrs Drew?'

'Joanna lived alone in a cottage down across the field. You can

16

see it from the back windows. She married, when young, and moved away to Kent. But on the death of her husband, she came back to Bath and, until recently, ran a small antique shop in Broad Street. She really did have a flair for it. Always picking up all sorts of bargains . . . Instinctive, I suppose. Tom was always saying how clever she was. They were devoted, you know. God knows what he'll do without her.' She pointed to a framed photograph that hung on the wall. 'That's Joanna at the opening of the our study centre, if you're interested. Back row, second left.'

A plain, dark woman gazed back at Elizabeth from the group of people assembled on a sun-filled terrace. Severe features, hair with all the ripples smoothed out of it.

'I gather she was up here visiting her sister-in-law on Saturday evening?'

'Yes.' Mrs Fleming's voice was almost casual as she said, 'Tom was away in London for the night. Apparently, she was worried about Jane's safety. She had walked up here to check on things and it looks as though she'd just come in through the side door when she saw something up at the Exhibition Centre. It was starting to rain, so she grabbed Jane's scarf – rather a distinctive Indian affair – from the peg as she went out and threw it over her head.' She moved the pen to the other side of the blotter. 'It may have been a case of mistaken identity.'

'You mean that Mrs Maddocks was the intended victim? But why?'

'For some months now, Jane's been the target of rather an unpleasant hate campaign. The Animal Liberation people. One of their awful tracts was found next to the body. I'm telling you this in confidence, you understand, to put you in the picture.'

Elizabeth sat back and let herself be patronized. That way, you could learn things that were rather interesting.

'The fact is, we've had one or two other spots of trouble. Jane's car scratched up. And shots fired at it one night in the lane.'

There was a minor distraction as a secretary came in with a tray of tea.

'I wouldn't like the job of keeping the Wetherburn secure,' said Elizabeth.

'It's pretty isolated. And with the woods all around . . . It appears that the intruder came up the back way across the fields and

17

through the herb garden. He trampled all the new beds we laid down in the summer.' Margaret Fleming seemed to have two quite separate sides to her face. The left one was sharper, thinner, so that when she turned to pour the tea for a moment, you had this witch-like presence in the room with you. The right-hand side was her house-mother profile. Smooth, smiling blandly now as she handed Elizabeth a Royal Albert cup filled with weak tea. 'Try that, would you? If it's too strong, there's more water.'

'It's OK,' Elizabeth said after tasting the brew. It wasn't, but adding water wouldn't make any difference to inferior brand tea. She wondered if Margaret had Scottish blood, if she saved pennies by buying floor sweepings.

'So what had Mrs Maddocks done to invoke the wrath of the ALF?'

'Jane's daughter Philly – by her first marriage – was enticed into joining the organization and committing certain foolish acts which got her into trouble with the police. Jane made her give them information which helped them infiltrate a local cell. It's been a tough year for her – and for Tom, too, of course.' There was a sudden brief light in her eyes that disappeared again as she said, 'He's a wonderful employer. But, of course, we work very much as a team at the Wetherburn.'

I wouldn't care to be in any team you played in, Elizabeth thought. Too damned domineering. 'It can't be easy for you with two of your team out of action. Three counting Mrs Drew.'

'Oh, Joanna only helped out unofficially. And though Jane is in charge of textiles and needlework, she also freelances as a journalist, so the biggest share of the daily workload falls on Tom. I shall be glad when he's back in harness again, of course.'

Elizabeth put her cup down on the edge of the desk. 'Didn't Mrs Maddocks do a book about Shaker Textile Arts last year?'

'She did. It's top seller in our shop. And she's been commissioned to do another one on Pennsylvania German Embroidery.'

'Sounds like quite a workload she's got there.'

'Yes. But young Tim Quennell – his father's our assistant curator – has been helping her with the research as vacation work.'

There was a short silence. Elizabeth smiled. 'The Wetherburn obviously likes to keep things in the family. They tell me that your husband works here, too?'

'He does.' A peculiar look crossed Margaret Fleming's face for a moment. 'Who told you that?'

'The lady who showed me up here.'

'Ah, yes.' Margaret Fleming's thin lips seemed to relax. 'My husband is a highly qualified accountant with thirty years' experience.'

'Really?' Now why would she want me to know that? Elizabeth wondered. Interesting . . . 'Were you up here on the night of the murder?'

'Dear me, no. Oliver and I are always gone on the dot of six. The murder took place a good three hours later. Actually, we went to the theatre that night. Rather a splendid performance of *The Recruiting Officer* – marvellous eighteenth-century costumes. Oliver's fond of Farquhar.' Abruptly, Mrs Fleming changed the subject. 'So . . . to get back to the lectures . . . You will be expected to speak from two thirty until four o'clock on a Wednesday afternoon. You'll have an audience of fifty or so ladies, including our guides. We encourage them to attend all our lecture courses, you understand, so as to boost their knowledge of the museum contents. After each lecture, refreshments will be served in Abby's Tavern, which is our reconstruction of an eighteenth-century New England ordinary.'

She unearthed a file with registration and attendance sheets and passed them across the desk. Elizabeth declined a second cup of the witches' brew in the pot and prepared to make her escape, chatting about this and that as she went, edging the conversation back, circuitously, via the museums of Virginia and Wedding Ring quilts to the subject of Joanna Drew.

Glancing at the photograph on the desk, she said in as bland a voice as possible, 'Mrs Drew and her brother must have been close, if she came back here to live after her husband's death.'

'Yes. Very close. Tom's putting a brave face on, but privately he's suffering a great deal.'

Elizabeth gazed out of the window at the fine old courtyard. 'How odd to see your childhood home turned into a museum . . .'

'I suppose so, though –' Margaret Fleming broke off. The door from the inner office was opening. A man emerged, flapping the pockets of his heavy tweed jacket, feeling for something he had evidently lost. Rather an elegant man with thick, silver hair and very blue eyes.

'Margaret, have you seen my –'

'Not now, Oliver.' Margaret shut him up with a wave of the hand. 'I'm busy. Give me five minutes.'

'Oh, sorry.'

He disappeared again, looking humble and contrite.

Guess who wears the trousers in that household, Elizabeth thought. Bossy female, henpecked husband. Why on earth did she want to get rid of him with such urgency? Why didn't she want me to talk to him? Or vice versa.

3

'Quilts can tell you a lot about the women who made them. Or the gentlemen, as the case may be. Oh, yes – you'd be surprised. Amos Pulaski, from my home town in Virginia, quilts all day alongside his wife, Mary. Back in the Thirties, they set up a small building firm together; Amos taught Mary plumbing and carpentry so that they could get their business off the ground. When they retired, Mary reciprocated by teaching Amos to quilt . . . Anyhow, take this Turkey Tracks that I've hung on the wall to your left. Note what the versatility in design and colour – the riot of reds and greens – tell you about the woman who pieced it. This was a joyous and self-confident female who knew her own mind and had come fully into her own as a person. The quilting is in shell pattern for common, everyday use. If someone could just turn up the bottom corner so that we can see the back – thank you kindly – you'll note the feed-sack backing, which tells us that there wasn't much money around when it was made in the late 1800s.'

There was a general rustle of interest from the ladies – and three gentlemen – assembled in the lecture room that had once upon a time been a stone barn with a steeply angled roof and solid rafters. Elizabeth stood at the front by the slide screen with her half-moons perched right on the end of her nose, her clear green eyes examining her audience with the kind of confidence that mesmerized. There was nothing on the lectern in front of her. Who the hell needed notes? When she was on the subject of her quilts, you could saw her leg off and she wouldn't notice.

Fat, thin, old, young, the ladies of the Wetherburn gazed back at her with a collective expression of well-bred politeness. They were all splendidly coiffed and colour-co-ordinated. Pretty dumb, probably, to talk to this lot about poverty, but she went ahead anyway.

'I'm going to pass around some photographs . . . hand-coloured enlargements of the aftermath of the Civil War in Georgia. These were unbelievably hard times. Those men who did come back to their families had no stock to grow crops from. The Union army had taken it all. Inflation had gone wild and Confederate money was almost worthless.'

In the third row, a distinguished-looking matron began to hunt through her handbag. She detached a boiled sweet from its noisy cellophane wrapping paper and popped it into her pink-painted mouth.

'Salt got so scarce that people dug up dirt from their smoke houses where the meat had dripped and put the dirt in the hopper to dry. Then they took the water that ran through the dirt and boiled it down to get the salt.'

The door opened and someone said, 'Oh, sorry,' in a clear, incisive voice. A slim woman in her late forties, brown bob flecked with silver.

'People cooked corn pone for years without any salt,' said Elizabeth. 'And in Georgia, they cook it that way to this very day.'

She wondered if the newcomer was ever going to sit down. A smiling woman in an impeccable cashmere sweater, she was now strolling down through the central aisle as if she owned the place. There was a spare chair at the end on the left-hand side, but she ignored it, choosing to push her way through a full row instead. 'Sorry,' she said in that penetrating voice. 'So sorry. Is there a seat there? Yes? Oh, wonderful! Thank you so much.'

'And yet, in spite of the poverty,' Elizabeth said with a hard-eyed stare, 'women still went on quilting, at night, in the thin light from tallow candles.'

'Would someone be so kind as to lend me a pen?' the latecomer enquired, scarcely bothering to lower her voice.

Elizabeth gazed at her with menacing firmness. 'Should I wait, do you think, until you've settled yourself down?'

'I do apologize. I didn't mean to disrupt.'

Like hell you didn't, thought Elizabeth, who recognized a self-publicist when she saw one.

21

'Laura was on form today,' commented Madge at ten minutes past four when she was taking Elizabeth by a short cut down to Abby's Tavern.

'Laura?'

'Your latecomer. Laura Eyton. Manages the Wetherburn gift shop. Never the kind to hide her light under a bushel.'

Or her quilt on the old bedstead, thought Elizabeth.

'Laura got divorced five years ago. Now she's married to the Wetherburn.' Madge's voice was good-humoured, but dry. 'She lives and breathes the place. Acts as if it's her second home.' As they came out of a long passage into the back hall, Elizabeth saw that the police had set up a makeshift canteen in an old scullery. The murder HQ, next to it, was a scene of fiendish activity.

'Cast of thousands,' Madge said cheerfully. 'Odd, because normally you can never find a policeman when you want one.'

They went through a door out on to the flagged terrace and past the herb shop. To the right, lawns stretched down to old stone walls and the bare outlines of espaliered fruit trees.

'The Mount Vernon garden,' Madge said. 'Wonderful in summer.' She looked both ways, to check that no one was within earshot, then said in the kind of voice that people use to clear the air, 'Watch your back with Laura. She's one thing to your face and another behind your back. Devious . . .'

'She's caused you problems?'

'Me?' Madge gave a snorting chuckle. 'Good gracious, no! I'm not grand enough for Laura to bother with. My woollies don't come from Jaeger.'

This was indubitably true. Elizabeth had had plenty of time to study Madge's attire. She wore the kind of ancient cardigan that, sooner rather than later, would turn into the dog's bed . . . if it hadn't actually been used as such already.

'Laura likes to think of herself as Queen Bee.'

'Really?' Elizabeth was making a frantic attempt to keep up with Madge, who was always yards ahead.

'She's been here longest of any of the guides. Prides herself on knowing everything. Knowledge is power, you see. And boy, does Laura like to exercise her knowledge!'

Elizabeth asked how many hours Madge put in at the Wetherburn.

22

'Well, we're closed on Mondays. And there's a rota. Generally speaking, we do a couple of days a week. Sometimes three, depending on illness. For most of them, it's a social thing. The Wetherburn ladies are quite a little clique.'

Madge came to a halt, still chatting on, and shoved open a door that led into an extremely warm room, with benches and settles gathered around pine tables. Elizabeth inhaled a provocative whiff of gingerbread and cinnamon biscuits. The dresser by the service till groaned under the weight of flapjacks and Tollhouse cookies and Devil's Food cake. One wall was lined with shelves that held skillets and heavy-lidded iron vessels; cornbread and spice jars and home-made marmalade. Madge quickly ordered tea and cookies and by the time the rush had started and the Wetherburn ladies had come pouring in through the doors, they were comfortably settled at a corner table.

'Did Joanna Drew attend the Wednesday lectures?' Elizabeth asked with some curiosity.

'Joanna? Sometimes.' Madge flipped some sugar into her tea and began stirring it with the spoon. 'She would have hated all these last-minute, cobbled-together lecture arrangements. Joanna was a very precise lady. A stickler for the fine detail. Almost fanatical, you might say. Drove you mad sometimes. She'd come barging in and set on you for the least little thing. A tart tongue, Joanna had. The only ones to escape that were her dogs. She worshipped her dogs . . . They never let you down, I remember her saying one day. Dogs are honest. You know where you are with them.'

Outside, at this time on a winter's afternoon, the shadows on the clipped lawns at the back of the house were long and low. Dusk was falling.

'Dogs and horses,' Madge went on. 'Joanna liked a flutter on the horses. It was the only little weakness she would admit to. Everybody knew about it, but nobody dared mention the fact.'

'So did she win or lose?'

'Well, between you and me, on a lot of occasions, the bookies came away laughing. You'd know if she had a bad loss . . . it affected her temper, which occasionally got way out of control. But then, her bank balance would stand a few losses . . . Joanna was a very wealthy woman. She and Tom inherited a fortune from their mother. I remember Jane once asking Tom if they could afford a new computer system, almost certain his answer would be something like, "Not on your nelly," only he amazed her by ringing the sales chap that same afternoon.'

The tavern was now filling up and suddenly there were chattering clumps of women milling in a loosely formed queue around the service counter. Drifting and settling with their Old Colonial teacups into every last corner of the room. The noise level had become shattering.

Madge's body leaned forward, drawn by the plate of cookies, with their cherry centres and sprinkling of nuts and oats. 'You'll like Jane. She can never do enough for you if you have a problem. Not enough of that around these days.'

Elizabeth leaned her crossed arms on the table. Her gaze was on the bluish landscape outside the window. On the frozen lawns above the endless fields of a winter valley. 'Did Mrs Drew have her dogs with her on the night she was murdered?'

Madge frowned for a moment. 'Yes. I'm pretty sure she did. Someone mentioned that she'd shut them up in the old pantry. Apparently, they made a terrible racket when the police car arrived.'

'Was she in the habit of walking her dogs in the dark? I mean, it must have been pitch black coming up across those fields.'

'I think she walked them most nights. I can't tell you which routes she normally took, but she knew the footpaths like the back of her hand. Brought up here, you see. And she was very worried about Jane's safety that evening. She had rung the Wetherburn at five to say that she'd noticed a man lurking in a van in the lane outside the main gates. She thought she'd seen his face in court. She wanted to know if she should ring the police.'

'In court?'

'Philly testified against one or two members of the ALF. The whole family attended.'

'So did Mrs Drew ring the police that night?'

'Apparently not. Margaret took the call – Jane had gone to her health club – and she told Joanna to calm down and stop making such a fuss. But she was still bothered enough to walk up here that evening.'

Elizabeth thoughtfully took a sip of tea. 'Did Joanna drive?'

'Certainly. She had a little Fiat.'

24

'Then I still don't see why she *walked* up in the dark. I'd have taken the car.'

'Me, too. But going around by the road would probably take longer. And if she wanted to quietly check the place . . . That's Joanna's cottage straight below us. By the trees, to the right of the stile. And that's Nick's place – Nick Quennell, our assistant curator – further down the lane. The house with the extension at the back . . . His wife, Lucy – lovely woman – has multiple sclerosis. It's all dreadfully sad. He had the extension put on for her, all on one level.'

Elizabeth sat there and gazed out at the darkening valley. There were lighted windows in the lower line of cottages, but not in that which had belonged to Joanna Drew. That grey, hairline crack down below the herb garden was the ha-ha – a long, low ditch dug in the time of the Regent to keep the sheep from wandering into the grounds. Better than ruining the view with hedges or fences.

Her gaze swung back into the bright warmth of the room. Focused on the ebb and surge of the crowd and the chattering voices. Three guesses what they were all talking about.

'Mrs Fleming says you have a good team at the Wetherburn. One big happy family.'

Madge laughed. 'A family? Is that what she called it? Tribe, more like. You're OK as long you do what the Big Chief says. Or the Big Chief's sister.'

'And now that Joanna's gone?'

'Now that Joanna's gone, there'll be a new pecking order. Oh, yes, quite different, I shouldn't wonder.'

4

New pecking order or not, Tom Maddocks' little flock came together, at eight thirty on Friday evening, for a fund-raising Cheese and Wine evening arranged by the Friends of Wetherburn.

There was no question of them pecking at each other tonight. None at all. Perhaps a little clucking and fussing among the hierarchy that was crammed into the Quilt Room. They were a mite more nervous than usual. Jittery even. But the necessary process of circulating socially – introducing yourself around with a timely word here and a nod of the head there, scratching around for the odd bit of conversation – would cure that.

Elizabeth was glad, on the whole, that she had brought Max along. For one thing, it felt good, at her advanced age, to be towing along so obviously a personable young man. For another, they could compare notes afterwards. Two heads, even when one of them belonged to Max, were indubitably better than one.

'Reuben Dando's been on the blower,' he'd told her earlier that afternoon. 'He's steaming mad about the Wetherburn attack. Wants me to widen the investigation. I thought you might like to come in on this one, seeing that you're up there working . . . and that you're now a part of the Shepard Agency . . .'

She had bailed him out, months back, when his office had been broken into and his computer stolen. The partnership had been by way of thanks for the loan she had made him. It was probably the only return she would ever get for her capital.

'So where's Tom Maddocks?' Max asked, refilling Elizabeth's glass with some uncommonly rough red wine.

'He won't be putting in an appearance. That's understandable. Madge says they wanted to postpone the shindig, but he wouldn't hear of it.' She went on studying the crowd. 'That's Jane Maddocks over in the corner. Cropped fair hair. Talking to Reuben Dando. You're right. He doesn't look too happy.'

'Would you be with the ALF on your back?'

Reuben stood with his back to the wall, a dark, glowering man in his mid-fifties, his powerful shoulders encased in a heavy tweed jacket.

'His wife's certainly under stress,' Elizabeth said.

As she spoke, Ruth Dando moved away from the long window and crossed almost regally towards them. She dropped her glass on the buffet table. Thick, dark hair caught up in a clip. Red silk jacket emphasizing her high colour.

'Are you responsible for this wonderful spread?' Max asked her.

Elizabeth remembered that Ruth ran a small catering firm with Katherine Ellerton, the new vicar's wife. Dinner parties and board-room luncheons. The classier end of the market.

'No, they don't come to us.' Ruth's gaze was unsmiling. 'Joanna always said we were too expensive.'

26

'Pity. I enjoyed your last one.'

'Where was that?' The set of her features was mask-like. Cool cookie, Elizabeth thought.

'The Bath Festival gig. Posh picnic with jazz ensemble.' Max flung her one of his five hundred watt smiles. 'You must have had a rough week.'

'A rough few months, more like!' Reuben Dando suddenly loomed from behind his wife.

'Pity you weren't up here patrolling the other night. You might have been able to do something about it.'

'If I'd caught one of the buggers, I'd have used my shotgun.' Reuben's Somerset accent was as ripe as a good chunk of Cheddar. 'Tom Maddocks should never have gone off and left her on her own.' A bronchial cough shook his frame. 'God knows what he expected her to do with bastards like that hanging round the place!'

'Call the police?' Ruth suggested with heavy irony.

Reuben gathered his breath into an asthmatic wheeze. 'Oh, yes! And how was she going to do that with bullets inside her? If they hadn't got the wrong woman –'

'I'd have been delighted . . .'

Elizabeth, standing closest to Ruth Dando, heard the comment that was muttered under her breath as she turned and walked away. Reuben stood there watching her with a lingering scowl on his face. He emptied his glass in one quick movement. 'My wife's being her usual charming self. Should be used to it by now, I suppose.'

Elizabeth pretended to study the stitchwork on the cotton Amish bedspread right next to her. Solid colours, dark blues and greens and a brilliant fuschia, shocking in its intensity. The quilts were slung on long poles, like a forest of great banners to be swung back and forth at will.

Fortunately, a new voice broke in and snapped the tension. One that she recognized.

'I think you should avoid the quiche, Oliver. Pastry's bad for you.' Margaret Fleming, leaning forward to reach the paper napkins, actually found a smile for Elizabeth. 'I'm trying to keep my husband on the straight and narrow. He had a heart attack a couple of years back. Just a warning, but he has to watch his diet. Oliver, come and meet Mrs Blair.'

Tall and lean, Oliver bent towards her, his blue eyes peering with

27

mild-mannered politeness. A bit different from Margaret, Elizabeth thought. Oliver wouldn't hurt a fly in a butter pat.

'Mrs Blair. Delighted to meet you. Splendid lecture. Not in Jane's style – quite right, too. Do your own thing, that's what they used to say at my old boarding school. Would have upset the applecart if you'd taken them at their word, but still . . . Can I help you to some of this pâté? I was fortunate enough to spend five years in America as a young man. Got terribly interested in the Cornish colony in New Hampshire. Ever been there? My family came from Cornwall, you see. My mother's side . . .'

Margaret, at this point, was called away to organize the draw, or she would, from the look on her face, have stopped Oliver's ramblings. Elizabeth found his manner charming. But he was not a relaxed man, despite his eccentricities. He had an irritating habit of asking questions without giving you time to answer them . . . like a bird hopping warily along a branch, never quite daring to land.

'You must find life quite different on this side of the big pond? I worked in Washington for a while. Adored the Smithsonian . . . Wonderful institution! You must have been there? Should like to have settled in California, but I was engaged to Margaret by that time and she didn't care for it there. My wife comes from Yorkshire, you know. Didn't care for all that hedonism. Unlikely we'd have stayed there, anyway, I suppose, because I had to come back for – Good lord, is that the time? I'm supposed to help with the draw . . .'

'You meet the most unlikely couples,' Max said, as Oliver took himself off through the crowd.

The room was filling up now, getting uncomfortably hot. Elizabeth wasn't surprised to see the place so packed or the atmosphere so charged. Speculation was clearly rampant, with everyone whispering about the murder, but no one wanting to be caught in the act. The scraps of conversation flying out from the background hum were more ear-catching than the usual cocktail party chatter.

'. . . two ram raids in Taunton at the weekend . . .'

'. . . she won't go out of the house now . . .'

'. . . once in the head and twice in the chest . . .'

'. . . the daughter needs a good hiding, if you ask me . . .'

Elizabeth peered past the Baltimore Album quilt with its fruit and floral motifs at a cluster of people standing by the fireplace.

Her expression suddenly changed. 'Don't look now,' she said, 'but that woman's bearing down on us.'

'What woman?'

'You'll see.' It was too late to take evasive action, so she fished out a smile that had almost reached full warmth before the Eyton woman's voice assailed their ears.

'Mrs Blair! I've been meaning to apologize for disturbing your lecture the other day. Unforgivable of me, but my watch stopped. I didn't have a clue what time it was.' Laura Eyton was wearing a pale designer suit, expensively Italian, and a serenely self-centred smile. The attentive little glance that she threw in Max's direction told Elizabeth why she had graced them with her presence.

'This is Max Shepard.' Elizabeth put her out of her misery. 'He's a private detective.'

'Really?' She continued to hold Max's gaze. 'Wandering around the place spying on us . . . Well, well. Tom didn't tell me. I must have a word about this.'

'Max is here as my guest,' Elizabeth explained. 'Not on official business.'

Laura gazed at Max as if she didn't believe a word of it. As her freckled hand touched her hair, the light from the chandelier caught her two twisted gold rings, neither of them on the wedding finger.

'Well, now that you are here, perhaps I can pick your brain. How can I stop these ALF thugs attacking my little shop in town? I mean, it's getting quite ridiculous. Three Mondays in a row, I've come in to find the locks filled with Superglue . . . and all because of a few leather bags!'

'Superglue . . .' Max didn't look surprised. 'Favourite ALF tactics.'

'It's bloody awful for business, as Reuben Dando will tell you.'

'Not a lot you can do,' Max said, 'except put someone on watch.'

'Which will also cost a fortune . . .'

'My services come relatively cheap,' Max told her.

'Do they, indeed?' Laura took a sip of wine and pulled a face. 'God, this is foul stuff!' She mixed the remains of her red wine into a fresh glass of white that she had taken from the tray. Obviously she liked to live recklessly. 'I shall also have a word with Tom about his vintner. But not for a day or two.' Her expression had softened. 'He's having such a bloody time at the moment.'

Elizabeth had seen that schoolgirl-crush expression before, on

29

Margaret Fleming's face. Tom Maddocks, it appeared, was popular with the ladies . . .

Laura leaned against the long window, her gaze flicking around the room. 'I see Nick's knocking back the booze. Have you met our assistant curator, Mrs Blair? No? Well, we can put that right. Come along . . .'

Elizabeth raised an eyebrow in Max's direction and did as she was told. Nick Quennell, who had just finished polishing his glasses on a paper napkin, looked as though he, too, would have escaped Laura's clutches, had he seen her first. He was fortyish, tall, with brown hair and watchful hazel eyes. Not unattractive, in spite of the 'Don't-bother-me-now' look on his face. Elizabeth had the feeling she knew him from somewhere. Possibly he'd been in the audience at the lecture. His face rang a sort of bell, anyway. No doubt it would come back to her later.

With little enthusiasm or apparent effort, Quennell responded to Laura's introductions and shook first Elizabeth's hand, then Max's. His perfunctory smile showed for the briefest minute before packing itself away again.

'Nick helps Jane organize our exhibitions,' Laura explained. 'Or should it be the other way around? You must forgive me, Nick. I keep forgetting how long you've been here. It's a shame they don't give you a higher profile. You really ought to make more of a fuss. One never gets anywhere in life without being a bit pushy. I'm sure Mrs Blair will back me up on that.'

Elizabeth was glad Max had his mouth stuffed with vol-au-vent. It meant he couldn't laugh or add his own pennyworth.

'You should know, Laura,' Nick Quennell said, draining his wineglass and setting it down. 'You're the expert in that particular field. And now, if you'll excuse me, I have to ring home.'

Half an hour later, Elizabeth was heading for the Ladies room on the ground floor. A glance at the plan of the house had revealed that it was somewhere down a long passage that led from the main hall to the back of the house. She hadn't told Max she was diving out. He was enjoying himself with the blonde girl who ran the herb shop and wouldn't have thanked her for butting in on a promising encounter.

The passage got colder as you left the public thoroughfare, and she drew her tweedy jacket more tightly around her. The plain tangerine-coloured walls changed first to a floral patterned wallpaper, then, as you went through a sturdy fire door, to a balding green flock. The piney polish aroma of the main hall fell away. So did the ticking of clocks and the harsh, intermittent rattle of the front door in the wind. There was suddenly an older, dustier smell of grubby skirting boards and dog and ancient pianos.

She went through one more door and knew, immediately, that she had gone wrong somewhere. A dado rail stretched from a table with a lamp towards a half-open door on the right. Behind it, someone was moving around and there were voices . . .

Two voices having an argument. The man, doing his damnedest to stay patient, said, 'Sleep up at the Exhibition Centre? Why should he want to do that?'

'He's worried about the exhibits.' The woman sounded nervously querulous. 'Some of them are worth a small fortune and if the ALF decide to strike again . . .'

'Unlikely, I should think, considering the police presence.' A chair creaked as someone got up.

'Well, all he keeps saying is that the insurance people are being funny. They won't keep the cover going unless we increase the security.'

'But what about Lucy?' The man sounded concerned. 'She can't be left on her own at night.'

'Apparently, Lucy's gone into hospital for a few days. Look – I think it's crazy for him to sleep up there, too, but you know Nick. He fusses like crazy and once he's made up his mind, you can't shift him. I'm sick of trying . . .'

'Allright, allright!' Patience finally snapped. 'Let him camp out if he must. I'd better walk the dogs.' He sounded unutterably weary.

Elizabeth's hand still rested on the dado rail. There was a short silence. She had this sudden, dreadful itch on the tip of her nose.

'I'll do it,' the woman said.

The itching was turning into a tickle. Elizabeth pressed a finger to her top lip. It usually worked.

'As you like.'

A door opened and shut. Elizabeth thought, she's gone the other way . . . The tickle had gotten inside her nose. Deep inside, where

31

it was impossible to reach. Without warning, an enormous sneeze shook her frame.

Too late to run.

The door suddenly flew open and a square-jawed, wiry man in a tweed jacket stood there glaring at her.

'Who the hell are you?' he said sharply. 'You've got five seconds to explain what you're doing here. After that, I call the police.'

5

'Oh, lord!' Elizabeth's response, in this emergency, was to ham it up. She clapped a hand to her forehead. 'This isn't the rest-room! I was looking for my coat.'

'No, it isn't. You're in the private part of the house.' Tom Maddocks' eyes shot past her as if to check that no one else was about to come bursting through the door. In his dark tweeds and regimental tie, he looked the perfect picture of your English country gentleman.

'I completely lost my bearings,' she said in her best Yankee-tourist manner. 'I am *so* sorry. I drank far too much of that *excellent* wine at your reception. My brain feels as if it went through a spin dryer.'

She saw him visibly relax. He said, 'To be honest, it's cheap plonk.' Then, 'You're American.' A light seemed to dawn. 'You wouldn't, by any chance, be my wife's stand-in?'

'Elizabeth Blair. Indeed, I would. And you must be Mr Maddocks.' She held out her hand. 'I'm so pleased to meet you. But so terribly embarrassed to have invaded your privacy.'

Tom Maddocks said, 'Think nothing of it. We've been meaning to thank you for taking over the lectures, but things have been . . . well . . .'

'I quite understand. I was so sorry to hear about your sister.'

'Yes . . . well.' Maddocks cleared his throat. 'You'd better have a coffee . . . if your head's spinning. Jane just made a fresh pot.'

'That's the best offer I've had all day. I could murder a cup of coffee.' Oh, God, Elizabeth thought. Put your foot in deeper, why don't you? But Tom Maddocks merely gave a grim smile.

'Don't worry,' he said. 'We could do with some light relief.'

To get herself out of trouble, Elizabeth went off at a tangent. 'Your mother was American, they tell me.'

'That's right.' He searched through the sideboard for another cup. 'She came from a wealthy East Coast family. When she married my father, she had a load of family furniture shipped across the Atlantic. It became the centrepiece of the collection when we opened the place as a museum.'

'I guess your Ma would have been pleased about that?'

A wry smile touched his face. 'Yes, but Father would have hated it. He was a bit of a Turk. A strict disciplinarian. My mother was the only member of the family he couldn't control. She had this Yankee sense of freedom, you see. She wouldn't give in to him, no matter how much he bawled her out.'

Now that he had relaxed, Maddocks had a breezy way with him. He was clearly used to trotting out the family history as part of the floorshow. He was a few years older than his wife, Elizabeth guessed, and his expansive manner would bore the pants off you if you spent too many hours in his company. But for the moment, he pushed aside his personal problems – with some relief, perhaps – to make her feel like an honoured guest.

Elizabeth said, 'I imagine it costs a fortune to keep up a place this size?'

'You're not kidding! We keep six full-time staff and thirty part-timers. They all have to be paid and then there's the structural maintenance. The roof of the west wing is under repair at the moment. You may have seen the scaffolding. That alone costs a small fortune. But I happen to think it's worth it. I couldn't let it fall to bits. The old place is so lovely, don't you think?'

He was right. The room they were sitting in was quite something, with its softly draped chinoiserie curtains and the fire halfway up the chimney. A shaft of light from the lamp caught the plum-coloured silk cushions and eighteenth-century panelling.

Maddocks apologized as he handed her the cup. 'It won't be as good as your American coffee.'

'It doesn't matter. I'm used to it now. Tell me about your mother's family. Where exactly did they come from?'

He gave her a long account of his American ancestors. He was, he said, terribly proud of them. His great-grandfather had been an itinerant fiddler who made music for weddings and dances all over the West. His grandfather had made a fortune out of pig iron and had built a great house in the Hampshires and spoiled all his daughters rotten.

According to Tom Maddocks, his mother had been rich, wayward and pitifully naïve about men when she had met his father one night at a dance on a wartime naval base in Baltimore. She had followed him back to England, where they married six months later because Tom was on the way. She had regretted the marriage almost at once, on discovering that her new husband had only married her because he had to rake up death duties from somewhere and that, far from being the strapping, warm-hearted fellow he'd made himself out to be, he was a tyrant and a despot who made his family's life hell and ruled them with a rod of iron. She would probably have legged it back to the States were it not for her children.

'I'm sorry, I'm talking too much. I'm probably boring you to death.'

It's shock, Elizabeth thought to herself. Always has to come out somewhere. Or is it that he's flattering me by giving me the lowdown? Trick of the ladies' man, revealing the old inner soul . . .

'I've been thinking about our childhood a lot these last few days. Joanna didn't have an easy life, you know. Not too many people know this, but she got pregnant by her boyfriend when she was only twenty. My father threw her out. Warned us to have nothing to do with her. But I wasn't having that. She came and stayed with me secretly – I had a house in town then – and somehow I scraped up the money for her to have an abortion. She finished with the boyfriend. Good thing, too . . . he was pretty useless. She made a brief, disastrous marriage a year or two later. But it didn't work out. Something about the abortion . . . well, more to do with her relationship with my father, probably . . . messed her up.

'Mother spoiled us silly. Joanna was petted and adored, but it was Father's love she always wanted and couldn't get.' There was an air of melancholy about the way he said it. 'We always stuck up for each other, you know. I remember once my father gave me a hiding and she actually went for him. I don't know who was more startled, the old man or me. Oh, yes, Joanna had a fiery temper when she was roused.'

34

'I did hear something about her going for Jane's daughter. At some fête.' Now who had told her that? Madge, probably.

'You heard that?' He looked startled, but lifted his shoulders in a brief shrug. 'Well, there's no use denying it. Everyone was there. The fact is, Jane's a sweet girl, but she let Philly get away with murder for far too long. And Philly embarrassed us all by calling Reuben Dando an effing murderer in front of the entire village.'

'Not terribly tactful.'

'I'll tell you something, Mrs Blair. Sometimes I think Philly's ALF activities were yet another attempt to draw attention to herself and make life as difficult for me as she possibly could. She's never accepted me as a stepfather, you see. She's unfailingly rude to me in public – ask anybody – but I try not to retaliate for Jane's sake.'

'That must put strains on your marriage,' Elizabeth said.

'Occasionally.' He shot her a sideways look. 'But nothing that we couldn't handle.' He picked up a photograph that stood on the table. 'That's Philly, taken years ago when she was on holiday with her father. He was a local vet. He died in a road accident when she was nine years old.'

'Difficult age to lose a father.' Elizabeth took the photo. The child had curly brown hair and she was leaning over a green rock pool and laughing. Love and trust filled eyes that were as blue as the sea behind her.

'Don't I know it!' said Maddocks ruefully. 'I suppose her love of animals came from her father. But he wasn't there to check it when it became an obsession. And I couldn't do it. She just wouldn't listen.'

Flames wrapped themselves around the logs until they spat half a dozen sparks up the chimney. There was a cold draught around Elizabeth's back and the springs in the chair creaked as she changed position to avoid it.

Quietly, she said, 'Do you blame your stepdaughter for your sister's death?'

'Philly's not mature enough to be responsible for her actions. No, I blame myself.' Elizabeth wondered how much more tightly his fist would clench. 'I should have been here that night . . . then Joanna wouldn't have felt the need to come and check. I don't know what I shall do without her, Mrs Blair, and that's the truth. Joanna was the brains behind the business . . . the bright one. She should have gone to university, but Father didn't believe in educating women. Always disparaged her. He'd have liked it if I'd gone up to Oxford, but I was as thick as a plank. Flunked every exam I ever took. Joanna never held it against me, though. She was so loyal. The best sister you could ever have. Got a bit too fierce sometimes, if you know what I mean. Had spats with people when she thought they weren't pulling their weight here. But it was all because she loved this place . . . loved me.'

Exhaustion suddenly seemed to have caught up with him. 'I don't mean to be rude,' he said, 'but I seem to have ground to a halt.'

'I shouldn't have stayed,' said Elizabeth.

'No. No, really, I'm glad you wandered in. It's good to see someone from outside. Jane and I . . . well, we keep going over and over the same things. Round and round in circles . . .'

He led the way back to the main hall, which seemed brightly lit after all those dim passages. The first guests were trooping out, beginning to leave.

A beam of light swung across the windows as they paused to shake hands.

Maddocks said, 'You won't mind if I leave you here? Only I'd rather not see any of them. I'm shattered.'

'Of course not,' Elizabeth said.

The swinging lights were from a turning car. Then a door slammed out in the drive.

'If you need anything . . . notes, books, samples . . . just give us a call. And thanks again.' He turned to retreat into the nether regions.

'There is one thing,' Elizabeth said. 'I was thinking about fixing something special for one of the meetings. Say, a quilting bee? Let the ladies bring in their own patchwork . . .?'

'Yes. Yes, anything. As you like –'

The outer door banged as someone slammed it. Maddocks' head shot round. Boy, was he jumpy!

'It's just someone's lift,' she said. Then, 'Is your wife going to be OK? Has she seen a doctor?'

'Doctor?'

'He might be able to help.'

'No. No.' Maddocks smiled stoically. 'She's coping.'

He turned to go, but as he did so, the main door shot open. A tall girl in a long, floral skirt erupted on to the scene, stood there, flicking her long hair back and gazing at the departing guests with what looked like venom. 'I might have known!' she said in a low, but penetrating voice. 'The bloody Wetherburn always has to come first.'

'Philly . . .' Maddocks moved towards the girl.

'That's all that you care about, isn't it? It's obscene, having shindigs like this when your bloody sister's lying down there in the mortuary. But then, I wouldn't expect you to know anything about decent behaviour. About actually caring . . . You're pathetic!'

The group at the bottom of the staircase had stopped in their tracks. Some of their faces registered embarrassment, others shock. Frozen to the spot, slightly off-centre, they looked like extras waiting for the next scene of the drama to unfold.

'Philly!' Maddocks' face was stern. 'If you've got anything to say, please say it in private. I don't want any more scenes.'

'When was this place ever private?' the girl asked. 'It's like Waterloo Station.'

'You could have come in the back way.'

'Oh, so I'm to use the tradesmen's entrance? Why should I creep around avoiding people? I suppose you're ashamed to have me around the place? You don't care to be seen with a common criminal?'

'That's not true. I can't trust you to behave yourself, if you must know. Other girls come home and –'

'Home?' The girl laughed. 'That's a laugh!'

Maddocks' jaw tightened, but somehow he was managing to curb his temper. In a steady, low voice, he said, 'Look – your mother loves you very much, but I won't have you causing any more trouble here. If you can't come and talk things over quietly, would you kindly leave the premises? Right now?'

What colour there was went out of the girl's face. 'Don't worry. I know when I'm not wanted.' Her expression showed complete contempt. 'I don't suppose my mother's interested, but you might tell her that I called. Remind her that I exist, if that's not too much trouble . . .'

The door banged shut behind her. Maddocks said carefully, in a controlled tone, 'Don't ever try and make friends with stepchildren.

It's a waste of time and energy. Goodnight, Mrs Blair. I'm sorry you had to witness that.'

'Who was it said that animals bring out the best in us?' Madge Radley asked as she lifted her coat from the peg and shrugged it over her sturdy shoulders. 'Mr Maddocks is too patient. I'd have knocked her block off. It's a pity Joanna wasn't here. She'd have sorted the little madam out. When she made all that fuss at the fête, Joanna sent her away with a flea in her ear. They had a real ding-dong in the middle of the lawn out there. Mind you, there were times when Joanna went too far. She got Tom into all kinds of trouble, over the years.'

'And what did Jane say to the scrap on the lawn?'

'Not a lot, on that occasion. Mind you, she didn't always let Joanna have her own way. If you did, your life wouldn't be worth living. Mrs Drew could be a holy terror.'

'So the two women weren't bosom friends?'

'They didn't get on brilliantly. But they were very different characters.' Madge searched for her car keys. 'And Joanna would try the patience of a saint.'

Max was waiting for Elizabeth outside in the porch. In the freezing darkness, a wind was rising. A gusty merchant that soughed through the bare boughs of the enclosing woods.

'What kept you?' he groused. 'I'm bloody frozen.'

'Poor old Max. Not used to females keeping you waiting?'

'Too right. Can you drop me off in town? I'm going on to a club. Special invite.'

What it is to be young, Elizabeth thought. All I want is my bed and my mug of drinking chocolate.

They said goodnight to Madge, whose car was parked very sensibly by the house, and started up the steps that led to the car-park. The Citroën sat up there waiting somewhere on the bare tarmac plateau. The rain which had been hanging around all day finally started to spatter down. It was turning into a filthy night.

'Get a move on,' she told Max.

'OK. OK. Got your keys?'

'In my hand.'

'Give them here. I'll drive.'

She was about to argue that she'd feel safer, thank you very much, if he didn't when a voice came echoing through the night. Max stopped so suddenly that Elizabeth almost walked into him.

At the top of the path, ten yards ahead, the blowing shapes of the trees were broken by two dark silhouettes. The man, cursing and swearing, was being restrained by a woman.

All at once, Reuben Dando . . . was he drunk? . . . hurled something that clattered down the path towards them. Before the faint light of the lamp was obscured by the branches overhead, Elizabeth saw that it was an empty tin can.

The red paint that it had once contained was now decorating Reuben's brand-new Rover.

6

'So Reuben wasn't best pleased?' said Helen, the following morning.

'Spitting blood, more like.' Max knew that he shouldn't be telling her about the paint incident. Client confidentiality and all that . . . But somehow Helen didn't feel like a paying customer. He found himself chatting to her about things that would otherwise stay locked up in his computer. 'There was paint everywhere. They'd smashed the windscreen and covered the car with paint inside as well as out.'

'Any idea who did it?' She gazed across at him with her amber eyes and picked at a loose splinter of wood on the desk in front of her.

'I'd take a guess . . .' Philly Lucas had to be the chief suspect. She must have passed the Rover on her way into the Wetherburn. Idly, Max wondered what it would be like to be Philly. An only child. No siblings to share your chafed feelings with, or your hopes and ambitions.

Weird, he thought. Can't imagine it.

He brought his mind back to Helen. 'I talked to the tenants in your husband's block of flats. One of them took in packages for him that were posted from a village called Hinton Bracknell.'

Helen listened attentively. He loved the way she listened, with that perfectly still look in her eyes. 'Where's that?'

'Buckinghamshire. And I was lucky with the bins.'

'The bins?'

'I went through the rubbish that he put out before he left the place and found this.' He rousted around his pockets for the relevant scrap of paper and pushed it across the desk towards her. 'I'm hoping you'll confirm that it's his handwriting.'

She picked it up and scrutinized it. 'Yes, that's Liam's scribble.'

'It seems to be a list of estate agents,' Max said. 'I trekked around all of them with his photograph and one of them thinks . . . only thinks, mind . . . that he was looking for rented accommodation a couple of months back, in or near Hinton. The girl got sniffy with me at that point. Couldn't release any particulars, she said. But I thought I might go up there and check it out.'

'Can I come with you? Please?'

Max shook his head. He'd have liked nothing better than an afternoon in the country with her, but managed to keep his libido under control. 'Better not. If he spotted you, he'd be off again. I don't want him doing that just yet.'

The joyous light died out of her face and left it apprehensive.

Max said, 'Tell me how much danger you think they're in.'

She was still outwardly intent on the splinter of wood. There was something about her that reminded him of Frances, his oldest sister . . . It was something to do with the long, fair plait, the deep frown between the arch of her brows. 'I wish I knew. I keep telling myself that he wouldn't hurt them, but if he gets drunk and loses his temper, he's liable to use his fists . . .'

Max wondered what he'd do if he found his brother-in-law beating up Fran or the twins. Kill him. There was never any excuse for violence against women. 'Well, if he's hiding out, I should think he'd keep out of the local pubs.' He came a decision. 'I'll drive up there this afternoon. Scout around a bit. I'll give you a call tonight. OK?'

'You won't forget?' she said as she left.

'Of course not.' You didn't let a woman like Helen out of your consciousness.

For whatever reason or no reason, Fran's image drifted vaguely in and out of his head all morning. The oldest of his three sisters and twelve years his senior, she had been like a second mother to him. She'd been known to call him a silly little bugger, but he didn't think she meant it. Max could always be sure of Fran's support, no matter what scrapes he got himself into. And there'd been a few.

Mind you, she never let him get away with anything. When she was good and mad she could give you a right bollocking.

When he went back up north, Fran's cluttered kitchen was his first port of call. He'd prop himself against the breakfast bar and wait for her to say, 'So how's it going?' And then he'd tell her. He could tell Fran anything.

'You're better off without her,' she'd said the morning after Jess had dumped him. 'Honest. You won't believe me now, but I'm always right.'

Was she? Trouble is, he thought, the feeling Jess had given him was not unlike a bolt of lightning passing through you. He hadn't set eyes on her since she'd walked out of the flat they shared in Manchester. It would be two years in December . . . He'd heard she'd gone down to London to do some modelling. Jess was always chasing after this job and that, running after the in-people who could help her career.

Max didn't think she needed much help. He'd loved the way she looked. Willowy and doe-eyed, but sensual.

'Not too many marbles,' had been Fran's opinion, though Max had always managed to shove the remark aside. He thought of something that hadn't really struck him when he lived up north (too close to it all, perhaps): he wondered if his family's coolness towards Jess hadn't been one of the reasons she'd gone off with another bloke. None of them had taken to her. Forward, Ma had said. Fancies herself, according to Rosie. But if they hadn't all been there, *en masse*, eyeing her up, well, perhaps she wouldn't have had to be so bloody defensive all the time.

All of which, of course, was water under the bridge. Max picked up the phone and dialled Elizabeth's home number. While he waited, he studied the pile of bank statements stashed away in the basket file on his desk. The last two left unopened. He didn't need to see them to know how much he owed. And the debit figure was always worse than you imagined. Why was that, when by the law of averages . . . ?

'Yes?'

'No need to snap my head off. I thought you said going home for lunch relaxed you?'

'Sorry, Max. The soup just boiled over, it's my lecture afternoon and I've just had the Church of Latter Day Saints at the door.'

'Recruiting?'

'No, they wanted to know if I had a Plan of Happiness programme. So what can I do for you, Max?'

'What's in your diary for Sunday? How about lunch at the Barley Wagon?'

'Great! Whose turn is it to pick up the check?'

'Er . . . yours, actually.'

'Ah, I see. It's the end of the month and you're skint. OK, Max, I'll feed you on Sunday. So . . . what's new on the gumshoe front?'

'Not a lot. I've been trailing Philly Lucas for Reuben. He's convinced she zapped his car.'

'And did she?'

'Not proven. All I know is that she's as jumpy as hell and acting very oddly. Two days now, she's parked herself in the street outside her ex-boyfriend's flat – chap by the name of Richard Nowak – or the toy and model shop where he works in Southgate. She never attempts to talk to him. Just follows him surreptitiously wherever he goes.'

'And you follow her. Well, that sounds a bundle of laughs. So . . . what time on Sunday?'

'One-ish?'

'OK. Book a table. See you.'

He put the receiver down. Picked up the top letter from the pile, the one he couldn't ignore. The one that said, 'Dear Sir, Be a good boy and contact us, or we bounce your next cheque.' He dialled another number and cleared his throat while he waited to be connected.

There were normally two females manning the desk at the other end. A pussy-cat that he could charm and an old bag who sounded as if she wore brass knuckles.

'National Westminster.'

Damn! It was Acid Knickers. Max jammed the phone back on the hook. He'd try again later, preferably after having a couple of pittas filled with chilli salad from Nick's Deli. Or a good pint of Pelforth to fill him with Dutch courage.

Elizabeth's second lecture, on the social aspect of patchwork, went pretty well. She spun them a bunch of yarns about quilting bees, interspersed with a few good gags. The Wetherburn ladies seemed enthralled. No one yawned or fidgeted.

Afterwards, in the Tavern, she sat in the corner settle resting her voice-box while flicking through the new guidebook she had picked up in the hall earlier.

The cover was attractive. A roundel showing the house in 1825 and flying ribbons enscribed with the Maddocks family motto: 'Leave no trace behind.'

Whatever that meant. The introductory blurb read:

> Visitors from all over the world come to admire the Wetherburn's 20 public rooms and our restaurant and coffee shop located in the old stables. We have recreated Sir Walter Raleigh's Roanoke Island Company and Jefferson's parlour. Indian settlements and the Booker Washington slave cabin . . . You will witness Abraham Lincoln's assassination as stitched into the red, white and blue of a patriotic quilt. You may drive a buggy around our pioneer farm. A day out at the Wetherburn is an unforgettable experience for the whole family.

Elizabeth lifted her eyes from the book as a splatter of rain hit the window next to her. Outside, the thick woodland was tossing in the wind. A single fat bird sat hunched in a tree down by the lake. A very cold bird with all its feathers ruffled by the north wind. OK, it was a rough day and someone had forgotten to put the roof on, but what the hell, he'd sit it out and wait.

The scaffolding outside the window rattled as the storm hit it. Something was swinging loosely from an outer strut. A rope with a bucket tied to it. There were no workmen in sight. They must have decamped in view of the weather and Elizabeth didn't blame them.

She flicked the page and continued to read. The tables all around her were filling up now, so that there was scarcely an empty bench or chair. But she paid no attention to anyone until a voice suddenly said, 'Well, you certainly know your subject. I'll give you that.'

Laura Eyton stood there gazing at her with a patronizing expression.

Elizabeth forced herself to smile. 'Thank you!'

'I don't know how you find time. I knew you ran a shop in town, but someone just told me you do a bit of sleuthing as well.'

'Part-time only.'

'Fascinating!' Laura continued to stand there. 'So who do you think killed dear Joanna? Any suggestions?'

'None at all, I'm afraid.'

'I'll tell you a secret,' Laura said, leaning confidingly over the table. 'It could have been any of them, in my opinion.'

'Them?'

Laura laughed. 'You're not with me. I thought you would be. Anyone who worked for her here at the Wetherburn.'

'What makes you say that?'

'Well, you don't seriously think it was the ALF?'

'No?'

'Not on your life, Mrs Blair.' She smiled as she leaned closer. 'They all hated her, you know. Nick, Margaret, Oliver . . .'

'Oliver?'

'Don't be fooled by that oh-so-gentle exterior.' A quick look round. 'Ask him about his regular assignations with Joanna, after hours. You might get something very interesting out of that. Oh, and ask him when he last had tea with Jane in town,' she said with a laugh.

Elizabeth watched her walk away down the aisle, jaunty and pleased with herself.

'Er – do you mind if I sit here?'

She glanced up with a start, to see Nick Quennell hovering a couple of feet away with a tray in his hand. He didn't look too keen to share a table, but it was the last free perch in the place.

'Feel free,' she said.

'Thanks.' He slid into the bench opposite and offloaded his tea and fruitcake. 'I see Laura got you. A word of warning. She's a bitch, to be avoided whenever humanly possible.'

'I think I'd already decided that.'

'Good. I enjoyed your lecture, by the way.'

'Why, thank you. It wasn't too folksy for your taste?'

He smiled. His eyes measured her. 'A little, perhaps, but it went down very well.'

'You're very tactful.' Elizabeth laughed. She hesitated for a moment, then said, 'They tell me your wife has MS. I wouldn't

44

normally pitch in like this, but I had an aunt who suffered from it. You have all my sympathy. It can be a cruel and relentless disease.'

'Yes, well . . .' Quennell took a quick sip of his tea. 'Lucy's been particularly unlucky. She's paralysed from the neck down and losing her speech.'

'I'm so sorry.'

'She was a brilliant young history student at Cambridge when we met. Lively and energetic. Threw herself into everything. But if you saw her now . . .'

'Tragic,' Elizabeth said. 'It can't be easy, holding down a full-time job and coping at home.'

'It's lucky that we live so close. I get a lot of the exhibition preparation done from home.' He cut his cake into three neat rectangles. 'When I can't be there myself, I pay a carer. And she goes into hospital now and then to give me a break.'

Elizabeth picked up the milk jug. 'It must be hard on your son.'

Their eyes met. Elizabeth wondered if she was misinterpreting Quennell's reaction. That he wished she'd brought up any subject in the world except that one. 'You've probably heard that Tim and I have a difficult relationship,' he said quickly. Too quickly. 'He was a mother's boy and his pain at what's happening to her comes out as anger against me. I should be able to do something about it and I can't. So little irritable rows blow up between us. Over nothing, really. Just sheer tension that comes spitting out of the air.'

She let him go on.

'Tim's never had a carefree childhood. I'm afraid it reflects in his character. He can be difficult and moody – or else, he retreats into his Walkman. But then, she's been ill for almost as long as he can remember and he's spent half his life silently worrying about her. He's always been aware of death around the corner, waiting to take her away from him. And sometimes, lately, I know he's wanted that. Seeing her suffer so . . . It doesn't make for the normal, happy home.'

'How could it?' Elizabeth said.

'In the sixth form, he went off the rails for a while. Drank too much, stayed out all night. Failed his A levels at first shot, though he's a clever lad. All due to the trauma about Lucy.'

Why was he telling all this to a complete stranger? Stress did funny things to people. Elizabeth said, 'They tell me you work hard. I expect it's sometimes a relief. Something to retreat into.'

'God, that's true! I bury myself in work when things at home get too bad. If you get absorbed in something, there isn't time to think. The Maddockses have been marvellous. Jane especially. She's a very practical friend in a lot of ways. She bakes me cakes. And she has this knack of steering people away when they start asking damn fool questions. You know the kind of thing. "How's Lucy today?" And you can't say that she's dribbling and incontinent and as unhappy as hell, so a head of steam builds up inside you . . .'

Elizabeth nodded sympathetically.

'And now and then it explodes. I'll blow up at somebody, simply because I can't explain how it feels. With an illness like Lucy's, you're up there on some dizzying drop, on some perilously narrow ledge, and it's as if people are shouting and waving to you from miles below and their words float up to you, but they don't reach you. You can't hear a word they say. An icy wind whips them away.' He seemed embarrassed, suddenly, by all the elaborate images. 'Yes . . . well. Jane steers people away. And I'm bloody grateful.'

'Your son must be about the same age as Jane's daughter?'

'Tim's a year or two older than Philly. They were friends for a while, before he went off to university.' Quennell started on the last segment of his cake. 'Philly used to come to the cottage when she was fifteen or sixteen to exercise Lucy's pony. It was someone for him to talk to. About Lucy, I mean. He wouldn't unburden himself to me.'

'So you didn't find Philly difficult?'

'Not at all. She's a nice kid underneath the show of aggression. She still comes up to read to Lucy and sits with her when I can't be there. Takes her out in the wheelchair sometimes.'

After a moment, Elizabeth said, 'So is your son enjoying university life?'

'I think so. He was glad to get away from home, and yet not, if you know what I mean. I suppose it's getting easier between us now that he sees it all from a distance. He's grown up a lot. Being away . . . having a break from the pain . . .'

Elizabeth steered the conversation into a new channel. 'I expect you could do without all this Animal Liberation hassle? Did Mrs Maddocks anticipate trouble on this scale?'

'No one could have foreseen it.' Quennell's face showed no emotion. 'I actually took her out to lunch on the day of the murder. A working lunch at the Barley Wagon, to discuss the photographic content of a textile exhibition Jane was planning. She seemed to be relaxing a bit more. Forgetting all the stress she'd been through . . .' He must have seen the look on Elizabeth's face. 'You're wondering why we didn't discuss the exhibition here at the Wetherburn. Well, Margaret's always trying to put her finger in the pie. If we were off the premises, we could talk more freely.'

'Mrs Fleming likes things done her way . . .'

'Precisely.' His fine fingers began fiddling with the knife on his empty plate. 'She's a bloody pain to work with. But that's strictly off the record. Not to be repeated.'

'I wouldn't dream of it.' Elizabeth gazed at him. 'I don't wish to speak ill of the dead, but I gather Mrs Drew could be a pain, too?'

'That's an understatement.'

'It's a dreadful thing to say, but I get the impression that not too many people will miss her. Except her brother, of course.'

'That's as may be.' His face sort of closed down at that point. 'I didn't have anything against her. Well, we had a bit of a fight about the extension I put up for Lucy. Joanna tried to stop me getting planning permission. She said it blocked her view. But it was nothing really.'

He was a bad liar. His face gave a twitch.

'And then she did block me when I asked for a rise in salary. If you make one special case for compassionate reasons, she told Tom, that's the thin end of the wedge.'

'Then you must have resented her attitude towards, you?'

He shrugged. 'All right. Yes, I did. But not enough to kill her, if that's what you're getting at.'

'Was Joanna intimidated by the ALF?'

'Mad as hell with them would be more accurate . . . the last time we met, anyway.' He seemed to stop himself and change his mind. 'And yet – and this is odd – she was suddenly very jumpy. She kept on about seeing this chap in the lane. She said she thought she knew his face from one of the ALF demos. And then, of course, she had the extra locks fitted and acquired one of those rape alarm things. Ellie told me.'

'Who's Ellie?'

'The cleaning lady that we shared. She did us both on a Friday morning, seeing that we were close neighbours. Ellie said there had been threatening phone calls to Joanna's cottage, as well as Tom's flat. Maybe that unnerved her . . . I don't know. When you live on your own . . .'

Elizabeth kept a bland expression on her face. 'So will her cottage go to her brother now?'

'I should think so. It once belonged to the Wetherburn estate. I doubt whether there'll be much more for him to inherit. She lost a lot when her antiques business folded. Joanna didn't know as much about the antiques trade as she would have liked you to think. She was a lousy businesswoman.'

'Mrs Fleming said she had a real flair for it.'

'Absolute rubbish,' Quennell said.

Then Margaret's either a fool or a liar, Elizabeth thought. But why would she deliberately lie about it? It didn't make sense. She saw that he was finishing his tea and shot one last question before he got up to leave. 'Were you around the place on the night of the murder?'

'No. I left early. Lucy was having a bad day. Well, none of her days are good, but this one was worse than usual. I had to call the doctor in the early evening.'

He brushed off Elizabeth's routine apology for keeping him gassing and went off to his upstairs office, leaving her to gaze into her empty teacup.

There was something about Quennell's attitude that bothered her. She didn't know what, exactly, but she couldn't get rid of the sensation that he'd been on the defensive, that there had been a strange smell of fear hanging in the air.

7

On Sunday morning, Elizabeth decided to go to church. A Sunday morning that was as fresh as pie. She dressed and ate scrambled eggs and drank half a pot of coffee, then shrugged herself into her warm tartan jacket. She had locked the door and was half-way down the path when Dottie Marchant called out to her.

'Going to Matins? Good. I like company.'

Dottie wore a voluminous wool coat that made her look like a badly wrapped tweed parcel. As she snapped her gate shut, she sniffed the cold air. 'Perishing, isn't it? I don't know about you, but I got out my warm underwear this morning. Viyella.'

'Nothing to touch it,' said Elizabeth.

Dottie walked with her head bent into the wind. She was wearing her usual Sunday perfume, a combination of lavender water and mothballs. 'How are the lectures going? And is there any news on the Drew affair?'

'Not a lot,' said Elizabeth.

'Of course, cruelty to animals isn't a modern invention,' Dottie continued, haphazardly. 'It's odd when you think about it, but Bernard Dando – Reuben's father – fired one of his workmen . . . threw him out of a tied cottage . . . for organizing cock-fights on his land.' Her round, green eyes looked more than usually abstracted. 'You never saw two men more different than Reuben and his father.'

'It often happens like that,' said Elizabeth.

'Bernard was a lovely man. Hopeless with money. But then good works don't often pay, you see.'

'Perhaps not financially,' said Elizabeth.

Dottie was silent for a while, then she heaved a great sigh and said, 'There were all sorts of theories about Bernard's demise. Most of them invented. People would rather pass round a tall tale than the truth, that's the sad fact of it.'

Elizabeth took it that she was supposed to ask. 'How did Bernard Dando die?'

Dottie stopped at the lych-gate. 'Hanged himself,' she said, 'in the barn one night. It was Reuben who found him.'

'Tragic.'

'Very. I feel sorry for Reuben sometimes. He was a handsome boy when young, but clumsy and shy. Carried a shine for Jane Masters, as she was then, but she went off and married the young vet. Building up the business and making money was some compensation to him, I suppose.'

But not deep down inside, Elizabeth thought. Aggression often stems from lack of love.

49

The congregation was small that morning. Fifteen or so hardy souls, not counting the stone angels up on the carved arches. Elizabeth sat in the third pew from the back and surveyed the congregation. The new vicar's wife, Katharine Ellerton, smallish and lean in her grey wool jacket, stared in the direction of the choir stalls and sang:

> 'Dear Lord and Father of mankind,
> Forgive our foolish ways . . .'

Her hair was cropped and discreetly burnished. She looked as if she would be more at home with a gin and tonic in her hand than a glass of communion wine. But did that matter these days? Probably not, Elizabeth thought. In England, where everything and nothing changed, it was perfectly understood that a clergyman's wife could have a few little sins like anybody else without too much harm done.

The Reverend Simon Ellerton was very young, with brown floppy hair. He wore his best Gentle Jesus expression as he raised his eyes to Heaven and intoned:

> 'Drop Thy still dews of quietness,
> Till all our strivings cease;
> Take from our souls the strain and stress . . .'

His cheeks were tinged pale pink by the stained glass in the east window. It was common knowledge in the village that he had little experience of leading a flock and was no match for his more worldly, feminist wife, who gave him a tanking every morning at breakfast.

Elizabeth finished the verse with him in a steady, low contralto:

> 'And let our ordered lives confess
> The beauty of Thy peace.'

Then wondered if, having put the washing in the machine, she'd remembered to switch it on before charging out of the door.

The text for the sermon was: Man, half-way between the beasts and the angels. Elizabeth sat in her pew seeming to listen as she admired the great bronze chrysanthemums behind the stone pillar. Their scent was earthy and musky. A warm draught from the underfloor heating hovered comfortingly around her left leg.

The Reverend Simon leaned forward on his hands. 'The Greek word for firewood . . . as used here . . . would seem to prove our point. St Luke said . . .'

Heavy stuff, Elizabeth thought, but he was rather beautiful, in an effete sort of way, and had evidently put a deal of preparation into his sermon. There were more winding ribbons of logic, more subordinate clauses than you could shake a stick at.

Not like the sermons back home in Turkey Creek. She had a sudden memory of bumping into the three ministers there, while they were holding their monthly breakfast conference in the Burger King on the edge of what passed for a town. Uncle Preach, the Baptist minister, had been passing round his book of gags. What if they've heard them, Chuck Randall, the Roman Catholic man, asked. Listen, an old gag is a good gag, Uncle Preach reminded him. Don't knock it, pally. The Lord loves a good floorshow, just like anybody else.

The Reverend Simon's floorshow, it had to be said, wouldn't set the world alight. Elizabeth hunkered down on the hard pew for the duration, while Dottie dozed next to her. At last, a wave of animation rippled across the surface of the congregation. The last hymn. The great exodus. Roast beef . . .

The air outside was dry and raw. Even the gargoyles, one on each side of the porch, looked parky. The biggest one, glaring violently down from the top of the porch, reminded Elizabeth of Reuben Dando. She wondered if it was a portrait of some distant ancestor of his.

Someone touched her on the shoulder. It was Katharine Ellerton. 'We wondered if you'd be free to come to dinner on Friday week?' she asked briskly. 'You'll know everyone, I think. Ruth and Reuben. Plus the Flemings from the Wetherburn. I've been meaning to ask you for ages. Oh, and by the way, is there the *slightest* chance that you might donate a piece of patchwork – something simple and inexpensive – for the Christmas Fayre raffle? Something attractive enough to take the central place in the display stand? It would be a splendid advertisement for *Martha Washington*, of course, as well as a rip-roaring fund-raiser for the Albanian Orphanage Appeal.'

Katherine Ellerton wasn't the kind to take a refusal. Elizabeth found herself accepting both requests with slightly mixed feelings.

Katherine hustled off, perpetually busy, perpetually talking. Dottie delivered judgement on her with alacrity. 'My dear, she doesn't send her children to the local school and sometimes her curtains are left drawn until teatime! Bring back Eleanor Silk, I say!'

Max was already installed at a corner table when Elizabeth walked into the Barley Wagon. Arnold was behind the bar. 'Drinks are free today,' he said by way of a greeting.

'Really?

Arnold winked. 'So long as you've lived in the village for seventy-five years.'

'Oh, right.' It was one of Arnold's little jokes.

'And you bring both parents with you to vouch for it.'

Arnold, the wag.

'Bottle of your usual, Mrs Blair?' he said. 'Because it's Sunday.'

'A bottle of my usual, Arnold. That would be just dandy!' He meant her favourite Côtes du Rhône. Arnold had her taped.

'No body to it,' Max said, when she poured him a glass.

Elizabeth ignored this pathetic attempt at humour. 'So tell me about Philly Lucas's ex-boyfriend. I'm curious.'

'Richard Nowak . . . Also involved with the ALF. He's a public school drifter. Travelled around a bit on the hippy trail . . . lived in one of those wagon things. Did some seasonal fruit-picking, in between the rock festivals. He has a two year old daughter called Poppy. Her mother disappeared and left the child with him when the relationship broke up. When Philly took up with him and he moved into her flat, she looked after the child.'

'And now they've split up?'

'So it seems.'

'And the child's with her father?'

'I don't think so. Haven't seen any sign of her, anyway. I'll have to go into that one, though it's probably irrelevant.'

Elizabeth studied Arnold's menu. She didn't feel like roast beef and two veg. The home-cured ham with two eggs looked tempting, but wasn't Sundayish.

Max said, 'There's another chap you might find interesting. James Lampard. He's a pretty powerful man in the local Animal Rights movement, though he claims to be just an administrative officer. Jane Maddocks hates him. She blames him for luring Philly and a lot of other youngsters into the organization and she's been doing her damnedest to find evidence that would land him in jail.'

'So he's a suspect in the Drew murder?'

'Well, the police hauled him in for questioning, but they had to let him go because he could prove that he was at a public meeting in Wales on the night Joanna was murdered. There were dozens of witnesses to prove it.'

'But he could have given the order and got someone else to do it?'

'Right. He's got a lot of fanatical acolytes. The cause is like a religion to some of them. Also some of the kids are fed speed pills at ALF parties. That was what first fuelled Jane Maddocks' suspicions. She found some stuff in Philly's bedroom . . .'

'So what does Lampard do for a living?'

'He runs his own financial advisory office in town.' Max eyed the rabbit casserole. He might go for it. 'He's a former tax officer. And a former organizer for the Fascist movement in Leicestershire. It grew pretty rapidly when Leicester became flooded with immigrants.'

'So he's Far Right . . .?'

'Mmn. The ALF's a good recruiting ground for the Fascists. There's a big pool of idealistic young people.'

'I wouldn't have thought them the same type.'

'Ah, but think about it. The neo Nazis home cleverly in on ritual slaughter in the Jewish and Muslim religions. They use it to promote anti-Semitic and anti-Muslim propaganda and encourage acts of violence. Also, Lampard's thugs have a sophisticated fundraising operation that milks the softer end of the Animal Rights organization for cash.'

'So tell me about the ALF set-up. Its structure . . .'

'They operate in classic guerilla style in a number of loosely affiliated cells. Organize local commando raids on businesses and individuals on their hit list. First-time members are usually unknown to other cells and necessarily change as some of them are prosecuted and exposed. Plus there are one or two publicists, who may have been active themselves once, but had to give up after prosecution. Like Lampard.'

'I'm impressed, Max! You must have done some work on this,' said Elizabeth with some surprise.

53

'There was a bit of trouble last winter. I had quite a file on it.' He sat back and grinned. 'Arnold had aggro from them in here, as a matter of fact. A group of them were in here eating their veggie pies when they noticed the pictures on the wall in that corner. Take a look.'

Elizabeth got out her half-moons and went to investigate. The first print – a red-coated hunting scene – was entitled *In at the Kill*. The second print, an etching of two men with long sticks, on which was impaled a dead or dying otter, was delicately entitled *Sticking the Otter*.

She sat down again with a grimace. It was odd how you didn't normally notice the goriness of all those jolly hunting prints. 'So they objected to the pictures?'

'Wanted him to take them down.'

'And I gather he refused?'

'Too true. He's been receiving all sorts of unmentionable things through the post ever since. But Arnold's tough. He says they'll get tired of it before he does.'

'Ready to order?' Tracey, the barmaid, was standing by with her notepad. 'Here, my old man works at Tithebarn,' she said. 'And it isn't just Reuben they has a go at. God knows how many of the workers' cars have been done.'

'Done?' said Elizabeth.

'Covered in pig slurry and paint. There's all sorts of rules now that they has to stick to for their own safety. Don't talk to strangers who ask about Tithebarn. Don't give them Reuben's phone number or that of the NFU. Don't answer the phone with the name or the working area, just the extension number. All suspicious parcels to be sent to security. Denny says 'tis like working in Parkhurst.'

Elizabeth decided against the chicken pot pie.

'And what about that campaign against the Rentokil drivers?' Tracey had a putty-coloured face and a frizzed pony tail. 'This chap Denny knows felt his hands burning one day as he was driving through Bristol. They'd sprayed the interior of the van with acid. He was rushed to hospital.'

'Why Rentokil?' Elizabeth was baffled.

'Well, they'm mass murderers, according to the ALF. Responsible for the horrific deaths of mice and rats. Now – what can I get you?'

54

Elizabeth rather thought that she was losing her appetite. She ordered scampi and tried not to think of little pink bodies.

'They're not all wild radicals,' Max said when Tracey had stomped off with the order. 'A lot of them would surprise you. Elderly and quite well-heeled. Pillars of society, in fact.'

'You know what bothers me?'

'Go on.'

'Too many odd details that don't seem to make sense.'

'Such as?'

'Well, why would the murderer scramble up over the herb garden in the pitch black, when he could quite easily have come up the front drive?'

'Didn't want to be seen?'

'Come on. The woods would have screened him until he got right up to the house. And why didn't Joanna take the dogs with her up to the Exhibition Centre, if she spotted an intruder? For protection, I mean. Why leave them shut up in the back scullery?'

'Not enough time? She was afraid he'd get away?'

'But you pass the scullery on the way out to the Centre. I checked the other afternoon.' She'd also taken a look at the coat pegs in the back quarters that led to the Maddockses' flat. Lots of very practical headgear that Joanna might have chosen. 'All she had to do was lift the catch as she went. So tell me what else you know about Joanna Drew.'

'She was the kind of woman who knew everything – or thought she did. She ferociously defended her brother against all-comers. She was a nosy-parker, thick-skinned, acid-tongued.'

'A pain in the butt,' Elizabeth said. 'Take a look at the photographs of her some time. Dark hair, dark personality, dark clothes . . . Which brings me to my next point. Can you see her putting that rather gaudy Indian scarf of Jane's over her head?'

'It *was* raining,' Max said.

'Not that hard. I put the milk bottles out at about nine that night and it was only a light drizzle.'

'The light was dim? She was agitated . . .'

'Maybe . . .' Elizabeth didn't sound convinced.

'So what are you getting at?'

Elizabeth said thoughtfully, 'Well, I was just wondering if Laura Eyton could be right.' She told him about Laura's theory. 'If one of the Wetherburn "family" wanted her out of the way, the ALF threats would give them perfect cover. It would explain why she didn't take the dogs when she went out to confront the intruder.'

'I don't follow.'

'If she knew the person she saw through the window, she wouldn't think she needed any protection. She'd just charge up to whoever it was and use her tongue, as per usual. It makes sense, doesn't it?'

'You're saying that the killer had planned it down to the fine detail? He deliberately left tracks up across the herb garden?'

'To make it screamingly obvious there had been an intruder . . . Whoever it was nipped in and took Jane's scarf from the peg . . .'

'They might have pinched it earlier. I doubt anyone would notice.'

'. . . draped it over the corpse's head, so that it looked like a case of mistaken identity. It's all hypothetical for now . . . but it *could* have happened that way. I just have this gut feeling. There are all sorts of weird undercurrents floating around at the Wetherburn.'

'Nobody liked her. I grant you that.' Max hesitated, then said, 'I suppose we have proof that there actually *was* an intruder?'

'Meaning?'

'Meaning that if we're assuming that the murderer was one of the "family", the prime suspect would be Jane Maddocks. She *was* alone up there with Joanna.'

'Hmm. Hard to see a motive. OK, so Joanna was a pain, but you don't kill your in-laws because they're irritating. At least, if you did, the prisons would be full to overflowing.'

Max was thinking hard. 'She might have been having an affair. And Joanna threatened to expose her.'

'Hardly a killing matter, in this day and age. Adultery and marriage break-ups are two a penny. Anyway, if she was having an affair and wanted out of the marriage, she'd just go. Happens all the time.'

'Yeah. Anyway, Joanna had gone up there because she was concerned about Jane's safety. That hardly shows bad blood between them.'

Elizabeth looked at him.

'I'll tell you something. There's bad blood between everybody else in that place. It's real fun. Now, pour me some more wine.'

8

The broad, green valley had been narrowing ever since Elizabeth turned off the main road, and was still narrowing. Bare beeches and the odd rowan edged the dark-ridged slopes to her right. Now and then the wind caught the leaves from the ditch and sent them skirling down the lane in front of her.

She paused at the DRIVE CAREFULLY, TOADS CROSSING sign at the bottom of the hill – couldn't imagine that was Reuben's doing – and the rusting remains of a burnt-out car. Then accelerated purposefully up Elliots Hill towards Tithebarn.

There were two farms in South Harptree. The first, Church Farm, was run on traditional lines, with old-fashioned barns and grazing sheep and a battered tractor that chugged along every year to help at the village fête. Then there was Reuben's place, nicknamed Belsen by the local residents.

In the fast-falling November twilight, she could see why. It had all the appearance of a concentration camp, with ten-foot fences topped with barbed and razor wire; and remote control video cameras on perimeter towers and floodlights that swept the compounds inside. No more darkness – except for the unlucky birds inside the recent expansion of chicken sheds in the fields this side of the house.

As she paused in front of the padlocked gates, she noticed a track that led up across the fields from Tithebarn to the distant Wetherburn grounds. In between was an old stone quarry filled with stagnant water that, for a fraction of a moment, seemed both cold and menacing.

She sat there, imagining the banshee-like wail that would reverberate across the valley if you were mad enough to try and scale the fortress walls.

An old man in a parking attendant's coat shambled out of a kind of guard's hut to check her identity. 'I've come to see Mrs Dando,' Elizabeth told him. 'It's to do with her catering business.'

'Hang on,' he said. 'I'll have to check. Your name, please?'

'Elizabeth Blair.' There must be some private way in, she thought, for personal friends. Always assuming they've got any friends left. I mean, you couldn't go through this palaver every time you called to pass the time of day.

On the passenger seat next to her was the file of cuttings Max had given her to read. Sticking out from it, an article about battery farming that she'd got half-way through. While she was waiting, she continued to read:

Imagine thirty thousand chicks from the hatcheries in tiers of cages in the long, windowless sheds. Every aspect controlled to make them grow faster on less feed. Food and water fed automatically from hoppers suspended from the roof. Lighting adjusted according to research. Bright light twenty-four hours a day for a week or two, to encourage them to gain weight rapidly. Then dimmed somewhat and adjusted to a two-hour cycle, in the belief that they'll be readier to eat after a period of sleep. At around six weeks old, when they're grown so much that they're crowded – less than the area of a piece of A4 paper per bird – the lights are cut to reduce aggression caused by crowding.

Normally, chickens have a pretty stable social order. When feeding, they fall into a pecking order. Cram them together in battery cages and all that goes . . .

Let a chicken out and give it straw and the first thing she will do is build a nest. And then have a dustbath, another instinctive activity to maintain feather quality. She makes a hollow in fine soil, fluffs the soil into her feathers and shakes herself energetically to remove dust. She will try to do it even in a battery cage. When she finds that she can't, she'll get aggressive and start pecking . . .

Now this is bad. Not because it hurts the chickens, but because it costs the farmer money. Mustn't give them the release of fighting, feather-pecking, killing and eating each other! Solution? He nicks their beaks off. This used to be performed by blowtorch, but is now modified to guillotine devices with hot blades that can do fifteen birds a minute.

Sometimes, when they're going at it too fast, the bird gets injured. Result? Blisters in the mouth, burned nostrils. Bad again, because acute pain stops growth. Other injuries caused by battery breeding? Ulcerated feet, breast blisters and hock burns. 'Chicken bits' are often the remaining parts of damaged birds where the bodies can't be sold whole.

Workers are warned to spend as little time as possible in the sheds and wear a respirator. Nothing is ever mentioned about respirators for chickens . . .

'Right – it's OK. You can carry on.'

Elizabeth dragged her eyes away from this catalogue of horrors and shoved the Citroën into first gear.

The gatekeeper stuck his head in her window. 'Bear round to your right and you'll find the farmhouse.'

As the gates swung open, she advanced into a bleak concrete yard. The gates closed behind her again with a resounding clang. She kept on around to the right, as she'd been told, past custom-built offices, until she spotted smaller gates flanked by a pair of milk churns. The only symbol of life as it would have been in the Dark Ages, twenty or thirty years back.

Ruth Dando answered the door herself, drawing back three bolts and a chain as she did so. She was smaller than Elizabeth remembered and had evidently been baking. There was flour on her dark green smock top and on the tip of one flaring eyebrow.

'Hi! I don't know if you remember me? Elizabeth Blair. We met briefly at the Wetherburn do the other night.'

She paused, looking at Elizabeth carefully. She didn't seem to welcome the call, but politeness overcame that. 'Yes, I remember. And I enjoyed your lectures. What can I do for you, Mrs Blair?'

'Well, I was rather hoping to make a sales pitch. I hope you don't mind. Only I'm canvassing local businesses and it occurred to me that you might be interested in rather a nice line in appliquéd table linen that would enhance your buffet dinners? I took the liberty of bringing up a catalogue and one or two samples.'

Ruth stared at her for a minute, hesitating. 'I really don't know. I'd have to consult with Katharine.'

'Of course. You don't have to make any decisions now, but if I might just pin-point the lines I think might suit your purposes? I won't keep you long . . .'

Ruth let go of the safety chain, with some reluctance. 'You'd better come in.'

She put up all the bolts again and led the way through a low hall into a late Victorian turreted sitting-room at the back of the house. A basket of dried flowers stood in front of the Portland stone fireplace. There were mushroom-coloured Dralon armchairs and pale silk cushions. Not a chicken shed in sight. Instead, the view ran down across a distant field to a couple of cottages. Elizabeth gazed out through the french windows into the blue dusk.

'I didn't realize you had close neighbours,' she said.

'We don't. The cottages are summer lets. There's also a converted barn that we've converted into holiday flats.'

Elizabeth moved away from the windows. 'I was brought up on a farm. It's so different from what it was in the old days.'

'You can say that again.'

'It's the same back home. You have to diversify to break even.' Elizabeth placed her bag on the back of the sofa and unzipped it. She unwrapped a set of place mats with dinky little Carolina Lily borders and a more full-blown turkey red and white Goose Chase centrepiece that might encapsulate the spirit of the season.

'That's lovely,' Ruth said, her face lighting up for one brief moment, almost in spite of itself.

'It is, isn't it?' Elizabeth rifled through the bag for the catalogue. 'I could probably do you a nice discount, as you're a Wetherburn Friend. Which reminds me . . . that was a nasty business the other night. Your car, I mean.'

Ruth's face went blank again. 'That was chicken feed – excuse the pun – compared with some of the other things they've done to us. We've had letters threatening to disfigure our daughter's face with acid. One hoping that our grandchildren would be born deformed. A funeral wreath on the doorstep. Not to mention the leaflets they distributed to every house in the parish suggesting that I used tainted scrag ends of our poultry for my catering.'

'Pretty lousy,' said Elizabeth.

Ruth's eyes swung away to the window. 'We've lived with daily abuse from pickets with loudhailers, blaring out lies about us that could be heard up in the village. We've had vehicles tampered with, a generator damaged. In the last attack, they blocked off the lane one night and attached incendiary devices to our vans. Heath Robinson, the police said. Made from a petrol can, firelighters, candles and table tennis balls. But they blew the vehicles apart and destroyed the garage as well.'

'It must be costing you to protect the place!'

Brief silence. Ruth had picked up the Goose Chase, but was giving it no more of her attention than if it had been a tacky old chain-store item. Her thoughts were elsewhere. 'A small fortune. The insurance premium has gone sky high.'

Elizabeth let the conversation lapse while she spread several more designs over the sofa back, pointing out the sale items and searching out their prices in the catalogue. Ruth fished out a Mexican Rose and said, 'Sal would like that. My daughter. She loves those bright colours.'

Elizabeth said casually, 'I suppose your daughter must be about the same age as Philly Lucas.'

'They were in the same class at Holborne School.'

'That's the posh, fee-paying one in town? So does she live here at home with you?'

'Only in the vacations. Sal's away at the University of East Anglia. She did very well at school. It was rather embarrassing really, when Philly got consistently bad reports.' Ruth's eyes seemed to be quietly mocking. 'Jane always had trouble with her, even from the early days.'

Something occurred to Elizabeth. 'So was Philly involved in any of the attacks on Tithebarn?'

'She took part in several of the minor incidents. But Reuben didn't press charges. She came down and pleaded with him not to.'

Elizabeth glanced at her. 'I can't imagine a little firebrand like Philly doing that.'

'No, not Philly.' Ruth's eyes were hard. 'Her mother.' The silence stretched on. 'Well, I suppose it was a change from calling to chat nostalgically about old times.'

OK, so tread softly here, Elizabeth told herself. No eye contact. Busy yourself with the contents of the bag and look like some foolish old woman who knows nothing about anything. Shouldn't be too difficult. 'Mrs Maddocks is an old friend of the family?'

'Of my husband's.'

Now that was one hell of a difference.

'They were practically brought up together. Her father was the

61

local auctioneer. She was always in and out here, like one of the family.'

'Then she'll remember your husband's father.' Elizabeth was still on fragile ground, but in that case, you kept on going in case it cracked underneath you. 'Dottie . . . my neighbour, Miss Marchant . . . was telling me how tragically he died. And how well liked he was in the parish.'

'One of nature's gentlemen . . .' A new voice had decided to join the conversation. Reuben Dando was standing in the doorway. 'But hopeless with money,' he went on. 'My father was a sucker for a financial sob story. Always giving money away. Not like me, eh, Ruthie?'

Finally, she answered. 'Not if you can help it.'

Reuben pushed the door shut behind him. He was wearing an old blue cardigan and felt slippers. His eyes were red-rimmed and puffy and he was still wheezing like a battered concertina. Elizabeth recalled the relevant paragraph in Max's article: ' . . . symptoms of those who habitually work in chicken sheds . . . regular cough, sore eyes, asthma or bronchitis.'

'I'm not a sentimental man like Father. He shot himself because he feared financial ruin. Well, that only made me swear I'd make a going concern of Tithebarn. And if battery farming's the only way, the *modern* way, then so be it. When I think of free-range hens, all I remember are unpaid bills and mounting debts and Father's lined face. You can't go back to Thomas Hardy and that lot and I'm not going to try.'

'Sal might argue with you on that one,' said Ruth.

'Sal might turn her nose up at the battery business, but it paid for her school fees and her foreign holidays and all her expensive fol-de-rols!'

Ruth completely ignored her husband's last comment. She bent down and switched on the lamp that stood on the low table next to her.

'And you've got everything, every gadget you could possibly want, haven't you?' Reuben said belligerently. 'You couldn't run your business without them . . .'

'Gadgets!' Was that contempt in his wife's voice?

'I'll leave a few of these with you, if you like,' Elizabeth remarked cheerfully. 'Take your time. You know where to find me.'

She put the catalogue down on the table. Conversation seemed momentarily to have come to a halt. She waited while Ruth put by her choice of table linen, then decided to kick-start it by casting one more line in Ruth's direction.

'From what I hear, the police have drawn a blank about the Drew murder.'

She hesitated. She wanted to ask about Ruth's movements on the night of Joanna Drew's murder, but could think of no way of broaching the subject without causing offence or putting Ruth on her guard. So she invented a downright lie. 'Someone told me you were up at the Wetherburn with Jane that evening. Preparing menus for some do or other.'

'Me?' She stared at Elizabeth.

'Yes, I remember now. It was Madge Radley.'

'But I was nowhere near the Wetherburn! I was here in the kitchen all evening, preparing salmon parcels for the Round Table dinner. Ask Katharine. She rang me just before eight.' Ruth was actually gabbling, which was quite alien to her normal cool manner.

'Then Madge must have got it wrong. She frequently does. I've found that out during my brief spell up there. She's a lovely person, but she does gossip. And what she doesn't know, she makes up.'

Forgive me, Madge, Elizabeth thought, for I have sinned, but it's in a good cause.

She started to pack away her things. As she did so, she turned her attention to Reuben. 'I gather you were up there checking the grounds every other night but the one when the intruder struck?'

Reuben said, 'Sod's law. If the bloody deliveries hadn't gone up the chute – I had to take one of the lorries out myself – I'd have been up there. But I didn't get back in time.'

'You were back here by eight.' Ruth liked contradicting him.

He ignored her.

'I heard the door slam.' She wouldn't let it go. 'I thought to myself, he won't be in long, that's for sure.'

'Well, you were wrong! I was bloody shattered. I work all the hours God sends.'

'That's your fault. You don't have to.' She looked at Elizabeth. 'Sometimes I think he does it to get away from me.'

Elizabeth deemed it safer to change the subject. 'Mr Maddocks tells me they're short of hard evidence. I do hope they find a lead soon. He's such a charming man. And he's in such a state about the whole thing.'

Reuben's laugh turned into a cough. 'Charming?'

'That's how he seemed to me. I mean, he was so solicitous about his wife.'

'Then why wasn't he where he was supposed to be when she rang him for help?'

'On the night of the murder?'

'When else?' Reuben picked up his pipe. 'Jane rang the number he'd given her from nine in the evening until well after midnight. He was supposed to be dining with this MP he was sucking up to.'

'Maybe there was some fault on the line.'

'That's what he said, but she had it checked and there were no faults reported in the area that night.'

'His friend said the line was a bit dodgy all day.' Ruth said it pointedly, as if to shut him up.

'Well, he would, wouldn't he? That type stick together like glue.'

'You're just prejudiced,' she said.

He gave her a look that said he didn't care what she thought. 'I know what that bugger's like, pardon my French. You women find him charming, but you'd soon change your minds if you had to live with him for a bit. Ask Jane. She'll tell you.'

'Oh, at length, I expect.' As Ruth said it, she sounded sweet, almost jaunty.

Outside, a sudden splash of rain hit the windows. It was four o'clock. Even Mother Teresa, Elizabeth thought, would be hard put to find something good, something comforting, to say about this happy little household.

If the signs didn't say shoot to kill, then they certainly said take no prisoners . . .

9

The girl in the green fish tail lifted her locks and sang to the ocean. Her hair had been dyed yellow and she looked as if she'd lived a lot. Max watched the pub sign swing in the wind and wondered if the artist had been drunk when he painted it and how come a pub called The Mermaid had got into land-locked Buckinghamshire anyway.

Helen's hair was as long as the mermaid's and it was crying out to be touched, even under the squashy brown felt hat she was wearing by way of disguise. He should never have brought her. She'd caught him in a moment of weakness, ringing him last night when he was asleep in bed.

Do you mind me ringing so late, she'd asked, only the middle of the night was the worst time and she'd opened a bottle of wine and sunk half of it already and if she didn't know that somebody somewhere was doing something about getting the children back, she'd go mad and jump off the Suspension Bridge. Don't do that, Max had said and then, by way of reassurance, he'd told her he was heading up to Hinton in the morning and one thing had led to another and somehow, against his better judgement, he'd found himself promising to take her along. All the way up here, he'd been trying to persuade himself that there was some logical reason for this decision, like he needed her to identify the kids and the job wasn't just computers and statistics . . . But seeing how strung up she was, sitting there in the passenger seat beside him, knowing that one false move could bugger up the whole shebang, he knew he had done the wrong thing and was mad at himself for being so stupid!

Helen squeezed the paper tissue in her hand into a tight, hard lump. Corkscrewed it into her palm and then wrapped it round and round two of her fingers. The Virginia creeper on the pub wall was a knock-out, the winter pansies in the window-box were a dazzle of yellow, but she might as well be blind for all they registered. Max pulled the lid off the lunch box she'd dumped in his lap and unwrapped the first neat package. Cheese rolls with a topping of coleslaw. She'd cut them into neat, bite-sized chunks and wedged paper napkins down the side of the box. Now and then he got a hot whiff of the coffee she'd poured him. It was as hot as hell and a shade bitter for his liking. But there was something instantly reviving about it and, after a while, some of the tension left him and it felt OK to talk while they sat there watching the cottage three doors away from the school. The one with the blue door, next to the bakery.

'How long have you been watching the place?' she asked.

'Three days.' Not continuously. He had varied the place and time. And this afternoon, the company . . . Which was possibly the only argument in favour of bringing her.

'And you think they're here? Liam and . . .'

'I'm sure of it. You're not eating,' he said.

'Not hungry.' She was watching the cottage like a hawk. 'But there's no sign of them.'

'Not yet.' He glanced at his watch. Twelve fifteen. That was OK.

'What if he's spotted you? I mean, in a place this small . . .'

'He won't have spotted me. I'm used to this game, remember.'

A blue car drove down the main street. Drew in opposite the cottage. Changed its mind and moved on again.

'I used to live in a village like this,' Helen said. 'When I was little. My parents ran an antique shop.'

'So where are they now?'

'In Ireland. And yours?'

'My mother's in Manchester. I scarcely knew my old man.'

'Why's that?'

'He . . . left when I was two weeks old.'

'Really?' That got through to her. Distracted her for a moment. She turned her head to look at him. Max felt the full force of her amber eyes. 'Why was that?'

Good question. He stayed silent for a moment, then answered it. 'He was carrying on with another woman – one of a long line. Some kind soul shoved a note through our door to tell Ma I had a half-brother only six months older than me.'

A young woman with a dog – a beagle – came round the corner by the post office. In the rear-view mirror, Max could see her tugging at the lead. She was wearing a red quilted jacket.

Max said, 'I'm supposed to be the spitting image of my Dad.'

Was that why Ma sometimes looked at him with a strangely ambivalent expression? With a kind of reproach, as well as love?

'Luke looks like Liam.'

'And you wish he didn't?'

'Something like that.'

The woman with the beagle had met a chunky friend who was pushing a white buggy. They stopped to chat for a moment, then continued down the street together.

'So you never see your father?' Helen asked. She was asking more by way of politeness than anything else. Her attention was focused once more on the tightly shut door of the cottage.

'He's dead now. I visit my Grandad, though. On my Dad's side.'

'That's nice. What's he like?' Her shoulders were hunched up deep in her jacket, her expression vacant.

'He's great. I take him out for a pint when I'm home. Never dared tell Ma.'

'She wouldn't approve?'

'You know what it's like. Grandad tried to send her money once, but she wouldn't take it.' Why the hell was he telling her all this? Abruptly, he took the conversation back to Liam. 'Your husband's already a regular at the pub here. I dropped in for pint a the other night and heard him telling the barmaid he's just out of the army and looking for a permanent house in the area. Looking for a job, too. Anything within reason, but preferably to do with cars or mechanics.'

The woman with the beagle had stopped outside the school gates. And suddenly others were gathering there too. The road outside the school was filling with cars and now Helen had caught on.

'We're waiting for him to pick them up from school. Oh, God – let me get out!'

'No!' Max had her arm in a firm grip. 'We mess this up and the kids may disappear for good. Today we observe. Then we go home and do some careful planning.'

'If you say so.' Her arm had gone limp. It seemed to take an age, but she was getting the message.

'Good girl,' he said. They sat and waited. The church clock chimed. It was fast. Three minutes fast.

'I know this isn't easy,' he murmured, 'but –'

'Max! Look –' Helen's face had changed and she was leaning forward. 'The cottage . . .'

The front door was opening and a girl was coming out. A girl carrying something floppy with a mop of red hair.

'That's Leila's rag doll!' Helen said.

'Are you sure?'

'Yes. I made it. I'd know it anywhere. Oh, god, Max –'

'Stay calm.' Max could feel her shaking like a leaf. 'Just sit tight. Keep very still.'

'But who is she? The girl?'

'She's supposed to be Liam's wife.'

The girl was in her early twenties, heavily built with reddish hair. She wore a baggy blue sweatshirt and washed out jeans and she looked confident as she shut the door behind her and set off towards the school gates.

The beagle had spotted another dog approaching from the direction of the church. He was going crazy, yanking at the leash so hard he was half throttling himself. The collar was cutting so hard into his throat, it was chopping off his frenzied bark. Turning it into the kind of cough you didn't like to hear.

Helen said, 'She's going to meet the children from school.'

'Right first time.'

The blue door opened again. A man stuck his head out.

'That's him,' Helen said harshly. 'Liam . . .'

The man had the door fully open and was leaning out to say something to the girl. He looked bad-tempered. The girl said something back, but he didn't bother to answer. Just shut the door again with a bang.

Max thought, I'll get you, you bastard, if it's the last thing I do.

There was the sound of a bell ringing somewhere in the playground and suddenly the scattered groups of mothers converged on the school gates. The girl with the doll disappeared into the crowd. Helen looked frantic.

'It's OK,' said Max, hanging on to her hand.

'I can't stand this.'

'Yes, you can.'

Her agitation was too painful to watch, so he kept his eyes on the school gates. The rush of escaping children carrying coats and satchels and things made from cereal packets was like a stampede of young calves. After a few minutes, the crowd thinned and car doors began to slam. The girl was still by the big gates. Still evidently waiting . . .

'Where are they?' Helen whispered. She was as white as a sheet and chewing on her lip. 'Luke and Leila . . .'

'They'll be here,' Max told her.

The beagle was towing his little party back towards the village shop. Dragging on the lead for all he was worth. It was starting to rain. And then two fair-haired children came trailing out of the school gates. The boy with his coat half on and half off, the girl dragging a bag.

'There they are!' Helen's face lit up for one moment, then went into a spasm of pain. 'Luke looks thin. And so miserable. Oh, *please* can't we take them now? There are two of us –'

'Too dangerous. Too many people around. And he's probably watching from the window.'

'But we'd be gone before –'

'No, Helen. Not today. You've got to trust me.'

They were walking back up the street now. The young woman trying to force Luke to talk to her, he resisting all her efforts to hang on to his hand.

It was true that he looked down in the mouth. Poor little sod, Max thought. It's always the kids who suffer. He saw too many divorce cases where the kids were angry and confused. Or in sullen torment. It wasn't bloody fair.

'He's taking one hell of a risk,' Max said. 'I mean, Luke would only have to drop something out to his new teacher . . .'

'You don't know Liam. Luke wouldn't dare.'

Helen was gripping the door handle. Max could feel her tensing as if for action. 'I know you're right, but I can't stand seeing him like that,' she said.

'It won't be for long, I promise.'

The girl had reached the cottage. As the children stood mutely behind her, the blue door opened as if by magic. So Liam *had* been watching and waiting . . .

Helen didn't make any sound as she went for the door handle, but Max leant over and grabbed her. Her breath made a rasping sound that was more desperate than any words.

'No,' Max said as he held on to her like grim death. As the girl ushered the children through the blue door and it shut tight behind them. 'We're not going to ruin things. We're going to beat him at his own game.'

She stopped fighting him at last. Stopped shuddering at the same time. Max went on holding her until the storm had subsided. Held her until she didn't move at all.

'It's all right,' he said softly. 'We'll win. You'll see.'

And then the phone went. The shock of it went through both their bodies. Max scrabbled for it before half the village was alerted.

'Yes. What the hell is it?'

'Max? It's Elizabeth. You'd better get back here pronto. There's been another murder.'

10

Long before you reached the Wetherburn, the still air transmitted a stench of charred timbers. A powerful and insistent smell of smoke lingered above the cars jammed into the one-way system in the lane, which was as close as the police would allow the public to get to the museum on this dreary November afternoon. There was nothing to be seen from the lane except for the grey pall hanging over the woods, making the winter sky behind the stable block seem pale by comparison. But the ghouls still loitered with binoculars and camcorders, hoping for a taste of whatever such nutters need to feast on.

The wall between the stable block and the main house was still standing, but it was black with soot and streaked with water from the high-powered hoses they had used to put out the fire that had destroyed the souvenir shop and half the store-rooms behind it. The bricks were still too hot to touch under the debris of the old cookstove that had once been such an attractive focal point of the Country Store. A twisted window frame, the colour of burnt molasses, lay on top of the pile of debris that had once been the till counter. Nineteenth-century pine panelling, brought over from New Jersey, had burned like matchwood at the height of the conflagration.

The charred remains of a body (female) had been found in one corner of the room that was used to store packaging, behind the shop.

Elizabeth had walked up from the village via the footpath that twisted around the edge of the woods and had struck out along a little-used track that led (if you hopped over a decrepit stone wall) to the grotto and the old icehouse.

She had half expected to be stopped by police or security guards. But on this south side, the grounds were deserted. She came up past the dovecote and the big monkey puzzle quite undetected and stopped to draw breath by a gap in the briar hedge that looked out over the herb garden.

Here the ground fell away so sharply down towards the encircling ha-ha that you could only see the tops of the trees and bushes above the south lawn. Round and round went the path down to the boating lake. Below that, ring after ring of fields stretched down to Nick Quennell's cottage. And the late Joanna Drew's. Beyond that, some three miles off, swept the long, honey-coloured crescents of Regency Bath.

The back terrace was empty except for a gardener down by the herb shop, who was yanking away at the dry vine stems on top of the stone wall. Elizabeth was almost within hailing distance of him when she was disconcerted to hear him call out, 'Bide there, you bugger! Bide there!'

'I beg your pardon?'

'Not you, missus. This'n.' He pointed with his secateurs to a freshly nipped stem that was refusing to stay where the knotty joints of his hand had wedged it. He must once have been a big man, but now his shoulders were humped and rheumaticky-looking. His feet were shoved into old gumboots and his shaggy head was as grey as a badger's.

'Oh, right.' Elizabeth watched him hunt for a piece of string. 'You've got your work cut out,' she said. 'I hope you have plenty of help.'

'Nowhere near enough.' The vine stem quivered as he grabbed it, then shot free again. From the look on his face, the air was about to turn blue.

She removed a sticky burr from her jacket sleeve. 'It's a bad business, this fire. Suspected arson, they said on the radio.'

71

'Aah. They said right.' His tone was as dry as the vine stem he continued to wrestle with. 'Petrol poured all over the place. Went up like a bomb . . . and thik Eyton woman with it. Mind, I can't say I shall shed many tears about the likes of her.'

'You didn't care for her?'

He spat on his hands. 'You'm right there, missus. Tongue like a viper, she had. They did make I watch this training video she were on. New-fangled nonsense! I told Maddocks, what dost think I shall learn from watching her prancing and preening? Thought she were in Hollywood, I suppose, with Marilyn Monroe . . .'

Elizabeth left him perched on top of the ladder. She went into the house by the back entrance and along the corridor . . . She had just opened the inner door when she heard Jane Maddocks' voice.

She sounded hysterical. 'I couldn't help screaming at him. I just can't take any more. What do you expect, with all this going on around us? It's like a bad dream.'

She was sitting in the stairwell, looking extremely distressed. Close to collapse. Elizabeth stood there in the shadows as Tom Maddocks tried, unsuccessfully, to calm his wife down.

'He only asked you where you were last night. He's only doing his job.'

'He knows perfectly well where I was! It was the police who made me go to Anthea's. Go and stay with a friend for a while, they said. And keep the address quiet.'

'But he had to ask you anyway. It was purely routine. That's what he's paid for.'

She collapsed on the stairs and started to sob. 'I'm sorry, I'm sorry, I'm sorry. But it's all so awful. This will close us down . . . You realize that? People will be scared to come up here at all.'

'Just the opposite, I should think.' There was a grim note of irony in his voice. 'They'll come to gawp, human nature being what it is.'

Elizabeth slipped back through the door. Went upstairs by a different staircase, a more roundabout route to the offices at the back of the house. As she passed the Flemings' office, Margaret caught sight of her.

'Mrs Blair! What are you doing here? I thought I told everyone not to come in.'

'Caroline must have forgotten to pass the message,' Elizabeth said without stopping.

Nick Quennell was sitting in his room with the door open. 'What a haven of calm,' Elizabeth said. 'They're all running round like headless chickens – oh, God, sorry – down there.'

'No point,' he said in his quiet, modulated voice. 'Work to do.'

He hit a button on his computer and leaned back in his swivel chair. Where *was* it that she had seen his face before? Months ago somewhere . . .

She noticed the large gold signet ring on his wedding finger. 'I expect you get used to dealing with emergencies?' she said. 'Plenty of practice at home.'

'You're right there,' said Quennell with a wry smile. 'Keep calm. Keep busy. That's my motto.'

'Did anybody see anything last night?' she asked.

'Ted Anderson was the last person to see her alive. He delivered some of those beeswax candles his wife makes. I was going to say they go like wildfire in the shop, but under the circumstances . . .'

'Better not,' Elizabeth said. 'Who's Ted Anderson?'

'Ageing hippy. One of your compatriots actually. He runs a shop called Avalon down in town. Sells crystals and Celtic runes and such. One of the gentler members of the Animal Rights lot. Friend of Jane's.' An odd look crossed his face. 'She went to him for information when Philly got arrested. He pointed her towards Lampard.'

'Interesting.' Elizabeth left him to his work, picked up a few papers from the cubby hole they'd assigned her at the end of the corridor and mooched on round to the Exhibition Centre, which had recently been reopened.

The bookshop in the entrance lobby was locked. She pushed open the swing doors into the main hall. Quite deserted. As quietly as a shadow, she drifted round the place, gazing at the maps of the Terra Nova in the glass cases. At the slim shelves that held Indian beadwork and Mexican pottery. The circus procession was still being displayed all along the far wall. A tiger in a cage was being drawn along by six dappled leopards. Three wooden clowns tumbled along behind and an Indian called White Hawk brandished his tomahawk in frozen fury.

Outside the double-glazed windows, the sky looked dim

and grey. Joanna Drew must have died just here where she was standing. Elizabeth remembered that Joanna was a betting woman and pondered the odds against her perishing in such an unlikely way and in such a grotesque setting. And now there had been another death just across the way. The two events had to be connected.

She had moved away from the circus towards the Columbus exhibits on the third wall when the door swung open behind her.

Elizabeth didn't know exactly why she gave such a start. It was animal instinct; nothing more. When she saw that it was Jane Maddocks, her heart stopped hammering.

'Mrs Maddocks!' she said. 'You gave me a fright.'

Jane stood there in the doorway. She looked as if she had recently splashed water over her face. She had certainly lost weight since the Cheese and Wine do. Her face, above a cream Aran sweater and greyish jeans, looked thinner. It wore an expression of weariness and indecision.

'I'm sorry. I didn't mean to startle you.'

'I guess we're all pretty jumpy.'

'That's an understatement.' Jane came forward and held out her hand. 'I think your lectures are wonderful. I meant to have said so before, but –'

'Don't apologize. There's no need.'

Jane said, 'I'm not really fit to be seen. I was escaping from Tom. He wants me to take a sleeping pill and lie down.'

'And you don't want to?'

'No point. You could knock me on the head with a mallet and I wouldn't sleep. Anyway, I have work to do.'

'You must be so sick of all this?'

'Yes. But it goes on and on.'

'Is it . . . was it the ALF?'

'I have no way of judging any more. Either that, or someone clearly wants to give that impression. There was a message in spray paint on the courtyard wall. LEARN TO BURN! I'm told it's one of their slogans.'

Which may or may not be public knowledge, Elizabeth thought. But if Mrs Maddocks had any suspicions about her colleagues at the Wetherburn, they were not apparent.

'What time did the fire start?'

'We woke in the small hours. Heard the slates popping. It was well under way by then. They think it probably started at about midnight.'

'But Mrs Eyton wouldn't have been working there at that hour?'

'We don't know yet. She told me she was leaving at seven. Tom checked just after ten o'clock and all the lights seemed to be off. But –'

Something was making her look even more miserable. 'What is it?' Elizabeth asked.

'Well, you may as well know. It'll be all over the papers by the morning. They think she was dead before the fire was started. So it looks as if she didn't leave the premises after all. And she wasn't just trapped in there.'

'Another murder?'

Outside, the sky was charcoal grey blending to hazy smoke over by the balustrade of the house. The room was strangely silent.

'I'm afraid so.' Jane's face might have been cut out of rock.

'Would you mind if I asked you something? I don't know if you've heard, but I work part-time for the Shepard Detective Agency. Your friend Reuben called us in. Could you tell me exactly what you heard and saw up here the night Joanna was murdered? It might help a great deal.'

'I don't mind at all, but I doubt if I can be any real help. I was watching television for most of the evening. I had no idea that Joanna was anywhere near the place. I didn't see or hear anything until I went into the bedroom at about nine thirty. The bedroom's on the the side that looks out over the Exhibition Centre. And there were lights on up there, when there shouldn't have been. So I went to investigate . . . and that's when I found Joanna's body.'

'Tell me about that – if it's not too upsetting.'

'The doors had been forced open – I presume that must have been the intruder. She was lying, curled up, just inside the door. One black moccasin half off her foot . . . Her hand clenched round a cage with a very yellow lion in it.' She shuddered. 'It was quite bizarre. I keep dreaming about it. One of the bullets had lopped off the tip of her left ear. It lay there on the floor . . . all bloody, with the gold ear-ring still attached to it. And she was wearing my scarf. I couldn't work that out. The place was a complete wreck and she was wearing my scarf . . .'

There was a little pause. Elizabeth said, 'Tell me about Lampard and your daughter. How did she get drawn into his organization?'

'Philly was sixteen when she got involved. She was an idealistic child. Impressionable . . . But who isn't at that age? It happened quite by chance. She was watching TV one night and she just happened to see a documentary about seal culling and it shocked her so much that she wrote a protest letter to the local paper. That's all it took. A week later, an ALF circular came through the letter box, with the date of their next meeting in town.

'I still can't believe she got in so deep and so fast. One minute, she was reading pony books and the next she was being questioned by the police about criminal damage. She'd broken the windows of a butcher's shop in town. And broken into some pharmaceutical laboratory in Bristol.'

'How did the police find out?'

'I told them.' Jane held Elizabeth's gaze for a couple of seconds. 'I found their instructions to her in her room. And I rang the police.'

Elizabeth was so startled by this that she said straight out, 'That took some guts.'

She said simply, 'If I'd let her go on, she might have got in too deep and killed somebody. It hurt me more than it hurt her, believe me! But I had to do it. Can you understand that?'

'Yes, I can. But I'm not sure I would have had the courage, in the same situation.'

'Yes, you would. If you have enough love for your child. The real kind, not the easy, superficial variety.'

In the eighteenth century, Orange Grove had served as a wide promenade with a grove of maple trees which would turn golden every autumn. Now, in the late afternoon, the Prince of Orange's obelisk was surrounded by snarls of traffic. Elizabeth sat in her car, gazing out at the hordes of shoppers spilling out of Sally Lunn's alley and heading back round towards the Abbey.

A gigantic turkey (was it the same one?) was parading down past Guildhall, handing out leaflets. A few snowflakes were falling, but it wouldn't come to anything.

On the other side of the roundabout, a newsagent's board caught her eye. The headlines read: WETHERBURN FIRE. MAN ARRESTED.

It didn't take much to nip out and buy one. The traffic wasn't going anywhere. Something had broken down up by the traffic lights. She climbed back in and slammed the door against the cold.

The leading article read: 'Richard Nowak, one-time boyfriend of Phillida Lucas, was arrested today in connection with the inferno at the Wetherburn Museum gift shop. Police say he is being held for questioning . . .'

11

Max strode up George Street and turned left up through Miles's Buildings to get to Philly Lucas's flat at the back of The Circus.

It would have been quicker to take the car, but he wanted to admire the Circus trees – planted in 1800 – and the fringe of Palladian back gardens and the wonderful cubist geometry of bow windows and Regency balconies and domes, of canted bays and stable turrets and stone paving slabs that everywhere abounded. As Elizabeth had once told him, there was nothing quite as beautiful as a good Georgian backside.

As he walked, his fingers toyed with the sheet of paper in his jacket pocket. A photocopy that his friend Andy had slipped him of the anonymous letter police had received naming Richard Nowak as Laura Eyton's murderer. Andy shouldn't have done it, but he was a good mate and Max would repay in kind when the occasion rose.

ASK HIM HOW TO MAKE FIRE BOMBS. ASK HIM WHAT HE CALLED LAURA EYTON WHEN SHE LATCHED ON TO HIS LITTLE GAMES . . .

The letter had been typed on cheap paper and posted in Bath. No fingerprints, no clues as to where it had come from, but the police had pulled in Nowak within the hour.

Philly's flat, listed in the directory as 11A St James's Buildings, took some locating, but at last he found it tucked away in an alley between a solicitor's car-park and a tyre servicing depot.

At a guess, the house had once been rather grander, but this morning it had a slightly furtive look about it. The paint on the door was scratched, the windows needed cleaning and there was a depressingly long line of bells underneath the dilapidated gas meter in the makeshift porch.

Philly was in, but she gave him a hostile reception.

'Why should I talk to you?' she demanded. 'Give me one good reason.'

'Your boyfriend's in custody. You might be able to help him.'

'Ex-boyfriend. Why should I help him? They can keep him banged up for all I care.'

Behind the wildcat words, there seemed to be a duller, more depressed reaction. She was wearing no make-up and her eyelids were red and puffy. Her black flares and scruffy blue shirt seemed hastily thrown on and might have come from some jumble sale.

'A friend of yours asked me to come.' Max took a wild chance. 'Nick Quennell. He's worried about you.'

An old look came into her eyes for a moment. Suspicion was replaced first by doubt, then a sort of burning intensity.

'Nick sent you?' she said. Then, 'You'd better come in.'

Her spine and shoulder-blades were still rigid under the thin stuff of the shirt. She led him up a flight of stairs and into a flat on the first floor. The furniture was of the usual student flat variety. Cheap moquette armchairs with throw-overs, plastic shelving and lashed-up curtains. A table in the corner was littered with an untidy jumble of papers and brown envelopes. On the wall next to the window was a huge, blown-up photograph of a beagle in a cage.

Philly saw that his eyes were drawn to it. 'Pretty, isn't he? They pump electric shocks into his tooth pulp to test analgesics. Now – what do you want to know? I'll give you five minutes.'

Max cleared his throat. His teeth were still jarring. 'Did you tip the police off about Nowak? Send an anonymous letter?'

'No.'

'Do you know who did?'

'I haven't the faintest idea. But I'm glad they did.'

'Did you know that he'd had a barney with Laura Eyton?'

'How could I? He's not in my life any more.'

'So you don't know if he had a motive for killing her?'

'I haven't a clue. I never did know what was going on inside his head.'

'Do you think he planted the fire bomb that killed her?'

Silence.

'Was it meant for Mrs Eyton, do you think? Or was your mother the intended target?'

'You tell me.' Philly bent to pick up something from the floor. A curtain of hair fell over her face, so that he could no longer see her expression. When she straightened up, there was a tiny plastic doll in the palm of her hand. She had fished it out from under the sofa.

Max decided to change his line of questioning. 'I didn't know you had a child . . .'

'I don't. But Poppy used to live here.'

'Poppy?' Pretty name.

'Rick's daughter.'

'How old is she?'

'Three. She'll be four next July.'

'Where is she now?'

There was a different note in her voice. 'She's with Rick's mother. In Yorkshire.'

Max unbuttoned his jacket. The room was stuffy and overheated and there was a funny smell that he couldn't identify. Might be coming from the dead flowers in the jug on the table. But then again, it might not. He caught a whiff of something faintly zoo-like. 'Have you got a dog?' he asked.

'No.' She gazed back at him. 'It's the rats that you can smell.'

Rats? Max shot a horrified look at the skirting board.

'They were rescued from a raid we did on some veterinary laboratories. They're in the kitchen. In cages,' she added, seeing the look on Max's face. 'Someone has to give them a home. A sanctuary. What did you think we'd do? Put them down?'

They locked eyes. Hers actually held a gleam of amusement. 'I feed them chocolate buttons for a treat,' she said. Then, 'It's the human rats I'd have put down.'

'Such as Lampard?'

'Among others.' Her gaze was dark.

'Were you up at the Wetherburn on the night Joanna Drew was killed?'

'No.'

'Or that evening?'

'No.'

79

'I gather you didn't exactly see eye to eye with her, though?'

'Did anybody?' Her blue eyes gazed steadily back at him.

Well, she had a point. Max decided to move on. 'Do you think Lampard capable of trying to kill your mother?'

'Easily.' Philly's gaze had gone back to the doll.

'So tell me about him. I'd really like to hear.'

He thought at first that she was going to refuse, but after turning the doll round and round in her fingers, she began suddenly to talk. 'He was nice to us all at first . . . at the early meetings in the church hall . . . like a kindly uncle. Gave us little talks with slide shows. Butter wouldn't melt in his mouth . . . but it was only to get us in so far that we were hooked. After a couple of months, he gave us this list of car numbers. People he said were involved in animal abuse. Then he provided us with paint stripper to use on their cars.' Her tone was contemptuous. 'He never touched them himself. He got us to do his dirty work.'

'So the paint on Reuben Dando's car the other night. Was that you?'

'No, it wasn't.'

'But you were up there?'

'So were a couple of hundred other people.'

There was another avenue that Max wanted to explore. He said, 'Your father was a vet, wasn't he? That's why you love animals.'

She shoved the doll away, clumsily, underneath a cushion. As if it was a symbol of something she couldn't bear to think about. She started to pick at one of her nails. Her fingers were long and slim and frail like a bird's bones.

'I wanted to be a vet, just like him. Only I knew I wasn't clever enough. I'd never have passed the exams. That's what *he* said anyway.'

'He?'

'My stepfather.' She said it with venom.

'You don't get on too well?'

'I hate him. She seemed to lock me out when she got married to him.'

'You might have locked yourself out,' said Max. 'That's what happens sometimes.'

'It wasn't like that. The dislike was mutual. He had my pony put down, just after Dad died. He persuaded Mum it had to be done. I wouldn't let them buy me another.' A look of triumph momentarily crossed her face.

'Wasn't that cutting off your nose to spite your face?'

'Maybe. But it didn't half make him feel guilty. Anyway, it was all right because Nick let me exercise Lucy's horse.'

She got up suddenly and crossed the room to stand by the window. It was dark in the corner where she stood. Her reflection was a feeble glimmer of blue in the glass. There was something in her eyes that was positively strange. Was she high on something?

'My mother didn't get married again, but I know how it feels,' he told her.

'Not to have a father?'

'Yeah. You feel a sort of failure. And it's not your fault.' He let the pause lengthen. 'And this Nowak didn't do you any favours, by the sound of it. Where did you meet him?'

'We went on an ALF raid together. I thought he was the cat's whiskers. Those sexy blue eyes and the smile he turned on . . . I fell for him because he seemed so at ease with himself and the world.' Another laugh. 'I thought it might be catching.'

Max waited for her to continue.

'Rick's a public school drop-out. He had a year making the tea in some solicitor's office when he left school. He was always quoting bits of the law at you, trying to blind you with his knowledge. Before he dropped anchor in Bath, he used to travel around in a wagon, picking fruit and such for a living. He could be fun when he was in the mood. He had this way of teasing you until you were under his spell. And then he'd let you see the other side of him. But by that time, it was too late . . .'

Poor kid, Max thought. Let down by one bloke after another. 'Things didn't go too well, then?'

'That's an understatement. The ALF suited Rick very well. There's a surplus of girls in their late teens or twenties, you see. And Rick fancies himself with the girls. He likes to cut a glamorous figure.'

'What did your mother think of him?'

'She hated it when I moved in with him. An out-of-work hippy, she called him.' She gave a wry laugh. 'And she was right.'

'And the child – Poppy – is the result of a former relationship? What happened to her mother?'

81

'Apparently she walked out. Took off and left the child with Rick. He said he was going to bring Poppy up exactly opposite to the way he'd been brought up. No sweat, no tears, no problems.' A hard laugh. 'At least, that was his story.'

She reached over to pick up something from the window sill. It was a balsa wood galleon. 'See this? Rick made it. He's into modelling. Spent hours at it.' Another dry laugh. 'He's good at assembling other things, too.'

'Like incendiary bombs?'

'Right. He used to make them so small they'd fit into a cigarette packet. He used to joke about it, when he'd got his stuff all over the table. Tweezers and torch bulbs and bits of old watches and tilt switches. One of these days, he'd apply for a job on *Blue Peter*.'

'Was Nowak was responsible for the fire raids in the summer?'

'Some of them . . . yes. He'd hide his devices under an armchair or a sofa on the top floor of a store, if he could. That way, when the sprinkler system was activated, all the floors underneath were flooded. Maximum damage.

'I knew what he was doing, but I refused to take part in it. I'd had my eyes opened by that time.

'Rick always found some girlfriend or other to help look after Poppy. Me this time. Someone else if I walked out. He never had any qualms about farming her out to the nearest woman with a tender heart. Or randy feelings towards him. I tried to look after Poppy for him, but the fact that she was being brought up away from her mother depressed me. It made me think more, this last few months, about the happy times I'd had with Mum. Made me feel sorry for all the things I'd done and said to hurt her. After all, it wasn't her fault that Dad died. These things happen.'

'Is this your flat or his?' Max asked.

'Mine. My father left me some money. Rick doesn't believe in owning anything. Property is theft, he says. He didn't even like Poppy having things. I used to sneak her in little treats I knew he'd disapprove of. I suppose that was the beginning of the end. When I started to criticize him in my mind . . .

'Like I felt sorry for his parents. I met his mother once when she came here and I liked her, though Rick always makes fun of her. He can be horribly sarcastic in a nasty, mocking sort of way. He had something against families. He loved to take the mickey out of what I felt for my father. He actually enjoyed it. I almost walked out that night, but there was Poppy to think of.

'I rang his mother now and then to tell her how they were. How Poppy was doing. He'd never bother unless it suited him or he needed something. He used Poppy as a sort of weapon against his mother. That was awful. He likes destabilizing women. He's an expert at it underneath that lazy, sexy surface.'

Just for one minute, Max thought she was going to cry, but she didn't. 'Why did it break up? Did he leave you?'

'No,' Philly said, 'I left him.'

'Can I ask why?'

Silence. She sat there chewing her nail. 'One day when he was out, I found his diary. It was a real eye-opener. He won't tell you things, but he wrote them all down. Nasty, derisive comments about me. And there were details about him sleeping with another girl. That was partly what made me take the decision.'

Max waited.

'Plus the night he took Poppy with him on a mission. That was the last straw. He went to lay some incendiary devices and he actually took Poppy with him for camouflage. He said no one would suspect you if you had a child in a buggy. That really made me see red. I mean, if anything had gone wrong, Poppy could have been hurt. I suddenly saw her future lying in front of her. She wouldn't have stood a chance. So . . .'

'So?'

'One morning, when we were supposed to be going to play-group, I packed her bag and I caught the train and I took her to her grandmother's house. I told her the whole story. And I left Poppy there.' A long pause. 'Nothing usually upsets him. He's too damned arrogant, but when I told him what I'd done – and why – he was as mad as hell. He hit me.' She lifted one finger to touch her eye. 'It's still a bit discoloured. When my mother found out, she waltzed in here and went for him. I thought he was going to kill her, but she told him to clear out and never come back. If he didn't, she'd ring the police and pass on everything I'd told her about his ALF activities. Dates and times . . .'

'So he went?'

'Yes. But you should have seen the look he gave her . . . He hates being ridiculed. She stood over there by the door and she called him an enthusiastic amateur. A rich kid playing at terrorism . . . which made him as mad as hell. I thought he was going to kill her . . .'

'Is he capable of it, do you think?'

'If the mood took him . . . He'd plan and bide his time, like a snake waiting to lash out and suddenly bite.' She was quiet for a few moments, then, fishing a crumpled tissue out of her pocket, she said, 'Do you know what I think? The terrorist activities filled a void in his life. He loved all the secrecy, the missions, the wearing of black and looking dramatic. But there was a coldness behind that velvety smile. You never got to know him. He wouldn't let you. I only saw his face really animated once. He was reading in the paper about somebody who'd been killed in an ALF explosion.'

And did he smile, Max wondered, as he watched the flames lick up at the Wetherburn? LEARN TO BURN! Yes, he could imagine it. But he didn't yet know where Laura Eyton fitted into the picture. 'He was a big admirer of Sinn Fein,' said Philly.

Max wasn't surprised. Lots of them were. Their eyes met. 'So . . . how do you feel about the ALF now? You must surely be disillusioned?'

'My central beliefs are the same. It's the people who are flawed, not the policies.' She sat there listlessly, the words seeping out almost in spite of herself. 'Some of the people in it were good friends, the kind I like being with.'

'One last question. I'm sorry to have to ask it. Was it possible that your mother might have been having an affair?'

'If she was,' Philly said, 'I wouldn't tell you. I've caused her enough trouble.' She added quickly, 'Look, we've had our bad times – mostly my fault – but I love my mother and I wouldn't want to spread any dirt that will make her life more difficult. Anyway, I can't see what her love life's got to do with these murders . . .'

Now that was an intriguing slip. 'You're assuming that Laura Eyton was murdered?' Max asked.

'It's what the papers are suggesting,' she countered quickly. She sat there listlessly gazing at the walls and the window and the Georgian shutters and at the buildings opposite. Suddenly she blurted out, 'Life doesn't turn out like you expect it to, does it?'

'Not always.' Max felt a great surge of compassion.

Her face screwed up like a baby's just before it starts to wail. Then, 'I'm pregnant. I'm expecting Rick's child.'

'Does he know?'

'Yes, I told him. But he doesn't give a damn.'

12

The shop called Avalon was packed with browsing customers when Elizabeth dropped in there to buy a birthday present for one of her nieces. Well, that was the story . . .

Some kind of New Age cosmic chant was softly emitting from the tape machine in the far corner. The blue and gold day matched the colours in Ted Anderson's shirt as he cruised the joint, chatting to his customers and sharing his passion for all things mystic.

'There's this very old wood behind our farmhouse,' he was telling a fat woman in velvet ski pants. 'It has magic vibes, you know? My wife goes and sits there when we want to start a child. There's something truly sexual about the place. You can feel it coming down on you. The trees, the air, the silence . . . Actually, we run Meditation and Inner Tranquillity courses out there, in the Buddhist tradition. Let me give you a leaflet.'

There were always mugs to be caught, Elizabeth thought, half-amused. She'd met Anderson's kind before, mostly around Walcot Street. Soft-around-the-edges hippies, but with a certain style to their well-spoken barminess.

Anderson sloped over to a boy who was studying the silver jewellery in the glass case. 'Have you seen the pendant carved with the celestial goose?' he asked. 'He's from one of the old Creation myths. Laid an egg on the Sacred Lake from which was born Ra, the Sun God. Friend of mine swears he keeps her inner flame burning bright . . .'

Flames . . . Elizabeth remembered the pathologist's report that Max had told her about last night. Laura Eyton had definitely been dead when the fire started. There were no traces of soot in her mouth or windpipe, so she could not have been breathing when the fire started. There was more. Examination of the lung showed fatty embolisms blocking the blood vessels – a sign of death by shock. And damage to the skull suggested a severe blow to the back of the head.

So whoever killed her had locked her in the store-room behind the Country Store, doused the shop in petrol, then hot-tailed it out of there after dropping the lighted match.

'Or there's the great god Min,' Ted Anderson was saying. 'A bestower of sexual powers on men. They fed him lettuce, did you know? Believed to be an aphrodisiac in Ancient Egypt . . .'

Elizabeth thought, junk talk has the same effect as junk food. It makes you want to throw up. Still, it was pretty easy to emulate. She picked up a small crystal from the shelf in front of her. Held it up so that the light caught its myriad angles and said in her most carrying voice, 'Grandfather Josiah swore by these things. He paid ten dollars for one – along with a milk cow – at the County Fair one day and you should have seen his crops the following year! They went straight up to the sun . . .'

'No kidding?' Anderson left the boy and came mosying over. 'Which County Fair was that? Where you from?'

'Virginia.'

'Know it well. Lived there for a while. So I guess you're on vacation?'

'Nope. I'm a fixture here. Intended to go home, but didn't.'

'Happens to a lot of us,' Anderson said. 'I had this kind of guru back in California and he said go to England. Find King Arthur. So I came over to see Stonehenge and to study. Don't you just love it here? It's less materialist . . . incredibly cool. And to live within reach of Glastonbury . . .' His smile was clear and meditative. It was charged with the sort of cosmic energy that needed earthing.

'You have quite a little business here,' Elizabeth told him. 'Must keep your bank manager very happy?'

'Tell my old man that, why don't you? He keeps on at me to come home and take the reins in the family firm back in LA. But it really isn't my thing.'

'What kind of family business?' said Elizabeth, being nosy.

He seemed embarrassed. 'Teeth, actually.'

'Teeth?'

'Yeah. Molars. My old man's a dentist. As a matter of fact, I started training to follow him, but I did a flit half-way through.

Couldn't stand the thought of staring at tonsils for the rest of my life. I still get phone calls from him, using the old emotional thumbscrews.'

'I get those from my kids.' There was a pause and then Elizabeth said, 'So you run healing and yoga sessions? That's interesting.'

'Plus weekend trips to sacred sites, and we own the health food shop in George Street.'

Quite a little empire, Elizabeth thought. Ted Anderson wasn't as wet-behind-the-ears as he made out.

'And you supply . . . or supplied . . . the Wetherburn shop, I hear?'

His manner appeared to shift. Suddenly there was a wariness in his blue gaze. 'Who told you that?'

'I work up there,' she told him. 'I heard you were a friend of Jane Maddocks.'

'Yes, Jane's a friend of ours,' he said after the briefest hesitancy. 'She often drops in for a chat. Persephone's a particular favourite of hers.'

'Persephone?'

'Our youngest daughter. Jane drops in to give her a hug when she's in town.'

'That's nice.' Elizabeth kept smiling. 'Shocking thing about Laura Eyton. I heard you were the last person to see her alive?'

'I didn't actually see her at all that night. I told the police. The shop was empty when I called.'

'What time was that?'

'Around seven thirty.'

'Did you usually call that late?'

'Sometimes. Anyway, I dropped the package I'd brought on the counter and left. Any more questions?'

'I'm sorry. It's just that working up there, you get caught up in it all. So do you know this Lampard guy? The big shot in the ALF? The one Jane had all the trouble with?'

'Sorry.' He stroked his beard nervously. 'My wife and I just run our own little group called Pagan Animal Network – PAN for short. Jane thought we might pass on some info about the parent organization, but I told her we're not into violence. We keep well away from all that.'

'Tough that the police searched your premises then, back in the summer?'

Max had fed her this interesting little snippet. Anderson was obviously disconcerted by this unexpected foray into his private life. He stood with his back to the crystals, a muscle in his cheek twitching. But he couldn't tell her to mind her own business without breaking his charm-the-customer rule. 'You and Jane had quite a chat! The police didn't find anything. We make tapes and run healing sessions and teach. That's all.'

'Tapes?'

'Music tapes. Womb music and Celtic pipes. We sell them in the shop and down at Pilton in the summer.'

'So did Jane ever come to any of your meetings?'

'She came along once, but it wasn't her thing. Anyway, that husband of hers objected. Told her it was a load of bullshit. Needs to let himself out of his strait-jacket, that guy.' A pause. Then a frowning question of his own. 'What exactly do you do up at the Wetherburn?

Elizabeth told him. 'I'm quite worried about Jane,' she said. 'There are such dreadful rumours going around the place.'

'Such as?'

'Oh, I couldn't tell you some of them. They're just too awful. People can be so very cruel and one shouldn't pass them on.'

'I can keep my mouth shut.' He was watching her carefully.

'Well, one thing doing the rounds was that Jane was having this wild affair.'

His reaction was totally deadpan. 'What's that got to do with anything?'

'Well, my dear, they were suggesting Tom Maddocks was jealous . . .'

'I still don't follow.'

'That he tried to bump his wife off under cover of the ALF threats.'

'Ridiculous!' Their eyes met. Elizabeth wondered if she was imagining the fear in his expression.

'That's what I said. I mean, she's not the type. They're obviously devoted.'

A longish pause. 'Of course, there *was* that business with Oliver Fleming. But Jane always maintained she found it embarrassing.'

'Embarrassing?'

'Well, Oliver had an almighty crush on her for a while. Male menopause, probably. He started dropping in on her after hours when Tom was away. Leaving little gifts in her room. Margaret wasn't amused.'

'I can imagine.'

'Poor old Olly. Should have been more adventurous in his youth, but he plumped for Margaret and lived to regret it . . .'

'So what happened?'

'Margaret put her foot down . . . *Wham*! . . . that's what happened. Stamped it out pretty darned quick. You won't find Peace, Love and Light on that woman's bumper sticker.'

Margaret stamped it out. Not Jane Maddocks. Elizabeth found that interesting, but she didn't say so. 'I'd like some literature about your farmhouse sessions,' she said. 'In case I decide to sign on for something . . .'

'Sure. I'll get you some.'

'Where is your farmhouse, by the way?'

'Out by Greystone Wood. Off the Wells Road.'

Only a couple of miles from the Wetherburn, Elizabeth noted.

'Come along by all means,' Anderson said when he gave her the leaflets. There was a blithe smile on his face. Seemed like he was glad to be on a safer subject. 'The times and dates are all on there. Give us a call or just turn up.'

Elizabeth went home with a Zodiac candle and a fistful of leaflets. She crossed the street by St Michael's wishing that there was some kind of geiger counter you could use on people. When you thought about it, Anderson seemed too much of a dipstick to be involved in anything sinister. The thing was, how much of him was genuine fruitcake and how much assumed for the purpose of selling his hippy merchandise?

She knows there is someone in the house. Not the nurse. Not the Incredible Hulk (Nick's name for her) clumping all round the place . . .

'Have a nice rest, Mrs Quennell,' she'd said. 'Buzz if you want anything.'

No, this sound is like rain spattering on hall tiles. This is new someone. A stranger. Came in on the back door.

By the . . . Words tangle themselves.

The soft sunlight of the afternoon has gone cold. Wind gone round to the north. When that happens, Lucy watches the maple tree outside her window. Three or four bright yellow leaves still on it, waiting to fall. November already. More dark coming.

The room that Nick built on for her is three steps down from the rest of the cottage; has new, white walls and sometimes it feels like you're on your bed in an underground shelter . . . waiting for next bad thing to happen. Not many more parts of her to break down. Most faulty already. Eyes, legs, fingers, arms. Paralysis creeping over her whole body. Can't scratch her nose if it itches. Soon won't be able to scratch her mind either. Bits of it are already detaching themselves from reality. Words, thoughts scattering themselves here and everywhere. Awful mess, Lucy. Tidy this mind up! It's in a dis . . . graceful state . . .

She dreams sometimes that the real Lucy's hidden under the mess. Wants to give it a good shake. Fling things around looking for her, but she doesn't seem to be there . . .

The sound comes again. Can't ignore it. Faint, like gravel trickling. Out there beyond the safe reaches of own room . . .

It's moving now . . . this way.

Buzzer, quick . . . Fingertip dead, but sweat breaking out.

Make words, then. Shout!

Mouth opens a fraction. Great roar comes out. *Ooo oow airrrh*!

Damned stupid sound to make.

Silence in hall, but the someone is still there. Where the hell's the nurse? Nipped off to the village like yesterday. Cow! Put the lamp on, somebody. Anybody. Oh, God, why can't I? Great, overweight seal, legs won't work, nor arms . . . Full of blubber. Only eyes will blink.

Bbbzzzz! Wires connect at last. Hers and electrician's. *Bbzzz*! *Bzzzz*! Loud as sin, but no one comes.

There comes, at this point, a whiff of something through the air. Something familiar. Perfume . . . after-razor. Definitely not nurse. She doesn't smell of . . . what? Lemon and musk. *Know* it . . . but can't quite place.

Lucy lies there on the bed on a day in November. Outside the window, the cold maple, winter's gloom, the rest of the world. And suddenly the fear lifts. She thinks: why worry about what this intruder might do to you?

90

It makes no sense.

Lucy would like to be a human again, only it's not going to happen.

So finish me off, why don't you?

Do me a favour. Do Nick and Tim a favour. Head back, eyes fixed on the shadow of the open door, she waits . . .

13

The woman in front of Max had a terminal cold and a bad case of pre-Christmas crabbiness. 'Kids get too much these days,' she remarked, slamming the cardboard box down on the counter. '£29.99 for a bag of plastic bits? It's outrageous!'

The shop was small and stacked from floor to ceiling with every kind of model kit imaginable – Oliver Cromwell, Norman churches, Superman . . .

'And then you've got to buy the batteries!' the woman said.

'I'm afraid it's gone up,' the assistant said, returning with the price list. 'It's now £35.'

'Then you can stuff it!'

The woman flounced out. Richard Nowak's expression didn't change. He put the box back on the shelf and said to Max, 'Can I help you?'

He was perhaps thirty, had blue eyes with pale lashes and he wore his fair hair scraped back into a pony tail. His face was still, on the surface, but Philly Lucas was right. The eyes were cold in spite of the smile. He had the look of a cool young Viking in a dark jacket that was expensive, but probably second-hand. Radical chic, Max thought, didn't belong in a scruffy modelling shop at the back of Southgate. And of course, Nowak knew that. Smug bastard, Max thought. Let's rattle your perch and see what happens.

'I certainly hope so. Are you Richard Nowak?'

'Yes.'

'I'm Max Shepard. I'm a detective. I've just been to see an old friend of yours. Philly Lucas. She thought you could maybe help with my enquiries.'

The smile was the first thing that hit the fan. Nowak's eyes narrowed. 'I'm working. If you have questions to ask, it'll have to be later. I'd be grateful if you'd leave.'

'I bet you would,' Max said. 'But I'm stuck here, mate, until I get some answers.'

'I spent half the night giving you answers.'

'You did?'

'Yeah. You're CID. I can spot you a mile off. Listen – I told you once – I was up at the Wetherburn the other night on purely private business and I was out of the grounds hours before the fire started. Mrs Maddocks confirmed those facts. Laura Eyton was seen alive after I left and you have witnesses who can confirm I was at Moles Club at the time she was murdered. So what the hell else do you want? This is police harassment.'

Max had to be careful how he reacted because he didn't want to let on that Nowak had just handed him a pile of fascinating facts on a plate. But no matter how convenient it might have been, he couldn't let the sod go on thinking he was the ersatz variety. Unfortunately.

'No, it isn't,' he said with a cheery grin. 'I'm the privatized version. Here's my card.' He enjoyed the look on Nowak's face as he handed it over. 'Philly didn't seem to know you were on hobnobbing terms with her mother. Odd kind of family this is. Can't quite make it out.'

'I shouldn't bother trying,' Nowak said. He had a slight northern accent. Leeds . . . the posh end.

'Oh, I don't know. It's all very interesting. Philly said her mother couldn't stand you. So what kind of private business took you up to the Wetherburn on the night of the fire?'

'You can get the hell out of here. I don't have to tell you any-thing.'

Max raised an eyebrow. 'No? Those incendiary attacks on Jolly's department store. Never caught anyone, did they?'

The snake-like gaze met Max's. If looks could kill . . . But the message had got through. 'All right. I'll give you five minutes. What is it you want?'

'What were you doing up at the Wetherburn on the night of the fire?'

'I had a phone call from Jane Maddocks. She wanted to see me.'

'What about?'

'Philly. The whole situation. Joanna Drew's murder.'

'She thought you had something to do with it?'

'No. She said she knew it was Lampard's work and she wanted me to help prove it.'

'Out of the goodness of your heart? Oh, come on!' Max didn't believe a word of it.

'The cow was blackmailing me,' Nowak said. 'She offered to do a deal. If I gave her proof of Lampard's involvement with ALF raids in general – and Joanna Drew's murder in particular – she'd forget to give the police everything she knew about my involvement with the incendiary raids.'

Lampard's head for his own. My God, Max thought, this is one determined lady!

'Why didn't she – or Philly – give the police this information earlier?'

'Why do you think? She'd rather have the power over me than hand me over to the police. Your secret's safe, she said, so long as you keep well away from my daughter.'

'Clever. So . . . you went up to the Wetherburn at what time?'

'Eight o'clock. She said she'd be on her own. The husband didn't know anything about it. I was to leave my car in the top car-park and walk down to the house. She'd be waiting at the side entrance.'

'And was she?'

'Yes.'

Max was desperately trying to remember the layout of the Wetherburn. 'Could you see the shop from the side door?'

'No. But the Eyton woman was still there sorting out new stock. Jane Maddocks had been round there at seven to tell her to pack in for the night. She'd have been happier if the whole place was empty. She didn't want anyone to see me.'

'Why not?'

'Well, it's pretty public knowledge that she considers me to be a nasty smell under her elegant nose. She didn't want to be seen associating, I suppose. She's a bag of nerves, anyway.'

'So could you give her what she wanted? Proof of Lampard's involvement in Joanna's murder?'

'I told her I could probably come up with something, but I needed time. The bitch said I could have a week.'

'So what story did you concoct for the police? I mean, you could hardly tell them the real reason you went up to see Jane that night. Not without incriminating yourself.'

'I told them that Jane hauled me up there because Philly was expecting my child and she wanted to know what I was going to do about it.' For the first time, a smile spread across Nowak's face.

'But Mrs Maddocks doesn't know that Philly's pregnant . . .'

'She does now.' Nowak leaned back and his smile widened. Philly Lucas had described it as sexy, but Max would have called it lazily vicious. 'The police are bound to ask her to confirm my story.'

Max eyed him with contempt. 'You bastard!'

He was still smiling. 'But I didn't kill either of those women.'

'No? But arson's your trademark. And the ALF have already had a go at Laura Eyton's shop in town.'

'You think I'm that much of a fool? No matter how much I'd have enjoyed firing the Wetherburn shop, I wouldn't have risked it, with Jane Maddocks on my back. Sorry to spoil all your neat little theories, but you can't pin that one on me, no matter how much you'd like to.'

The trouble was, he was probably right. Philly's ex-boyfriend was a right bastard. She was well rid of him. But, much as Max wanted him to be guilty, he could see the logic of Nowak's argument. And apparently, he had an alibi for the time that Laura was murdered.

Nowak was still grinning as Max walked out of the shop. The door jingled annoyingly behind him. Down towards the river, at the bottom of Southgate, gulls were wheeling and crying.

It was eleven o'clock when he got back to the office. He picked up the phone and rang Andy's home number. Lynn, his girlfriend, answered.

'Hi, Lynn! It's Max. Is Andy there?'

'No, he isn't! And there's no prize for guessing why not.'

'He's working. I thought he was off duty today.'

'They called him back on a case. Why did I have to pick a bloody policeman?'

Because she happened to be mad about him and they had this thing going, that was why. And she was also Andy's best mate and they stayed in and watched videos or went out together on matching mountain bikes and sometimes Max envied them like hell.

94

'Did he leave any messages for me? Only he was going to check on something.'

'Hang on. There's something on the kitchen table.'

Max waited.

'Sorry. The cat was sitting on it. Shall I read it out?'

'Might be as well.'

'Sarky sod. Right, are you listening?'

Max fiddled with his dictaphone and held it close to the receiver.

'Ready? It says: "Liam Weston. Nov 88, done for assault and battery. Fight in pub. Probation. April 90, complaint from wife. Beating. Hospitalized, but withdrew charges when she was discharged. May 91, suspected drug-pushing. Couldn't pin down. Fly guy." Hello, Max? You say something?'

'Nothing for your tender ears. Thanks, Lynn. Tell him I owe him one and I'll deliver tonight at the Star. Usual time, if you can spare him for an hour.'

He rang off before she could get in her reply.

A view down over tall, old houses to the floodlit Abbey in the centre of town. There was this enormous horse chestnut tree – all bare branches – swaying in the wind outside.

Max was sitting in the window seat, staring out at the winter night. He was trying to convince Andy that it was worth his while to pick up Nowak, but was losing the argument. Andy's case was that there wasn't enough hard evidence.

'We've known about him for ages, but we'd get laughed out of court.'

'Even with Philly Lucas's statement?'

'Pregnant ex-girlfriend who might change her mind at the last minute? Listen, I'm talking about material evidence. A good lawyer would say she had a grudge against Nowak and was making it up.'

'So you'll let him get away with the department store incendiaries?'

'We'll get him for something else, sooner or later. It's my round. Same again?'

Already Max felt as pissed as the proverbial newt. It had been a hard day and he felt narked that that slime, Nowak, was going to get off scot-free.

As the barman filled their glasses, Max shut his eyes and let his head flop back on to the comfortably plump plush sofa. For Nowak wasn't the only irritation that the day had presented him with. He'd been trying to contact James Lampard, only it was proving to be a thankless task. Lampard was never at his office when you phoned. The girl who answered the phone had a variety of excuses. Mr Lampard was either still at lunch or with a client or – interesting this – at his home in the country. And, no, she didn't divulge his personal number to prospective clients.

God knows how he made any money. But then, the office was only a front for his ALF activities. The money to run it was milked from other sources. Shifty and evasive, Max thought, but I'll nail him soon, one way or the other.

He'd left his name and phone number three times that afternoon and told the girl that it was urgent.

'Joanna Drew's bank statements were interesting,' Andy said when he returned. 'Quite large cash sums going in at regular intervals from an unknown source. Or sources.'

'She liked a bet on the gee-gees.' Max opened his eyes. A pervasive smell of steak and kidney was coming from the table behind and making him realize that he hadn't eaten since lunch. 'Maybe she had some good tips.'

'Nobody wins that regularly.' Andy took the froth off his beer. 'The brother doesn't know anything about it. She had no close family and precious few friends, it seems.'

So what else was left? Elizabeth's theory that Joanna might have been blackmailing someone. He tried the idea on Andy, as he reached for the menu.

'Joanna Drew was always nosing around the place. Suppose she had something on one of the Wetherburn family.'

'Someone who decided they couldn't afford to pay any more . . .' Andy was there before him. 'It's being considered. That's all I can say.'

'When did the payments start?'

'Almost twelve months ago.'

Max said slowly, 'And the second murder? It was murder?'

'Definitely. She'd put up quite a fight against her attacker.'

'No prints or anything?'

'All gone in the fire.'

Pity, Max thought. Old Andy was a handy contact and a good mate. Sometimes he gave you things deliberately (well, they knew they could trust each other) and sometimes he just dropped things out when he got tanked up.

The stuff about the payments was useful. It was all useful. Well, provided, of course, that you could still remember it next morning.

As it happened, he did. It may have had something to do with the early start. He got up at crack of dawn, well before the hangover could hit him.

By eight thirty, he was parked in the centre of Hinton, with Helen in the passenger seat. They had their backs to the cottage that Liam Weston had rented.

'You all right?' Max asked. She was very pale. The red wig looked incongruous.

'Panicky,' she said.

He glanced at his watch. Two minutes to go, if the kids were ready for school on time.

'Well, it's D-Day,' he said to Helen. 'You're quite sure now? You don't want to call it off?'

'No. I haven't gone through all this for nothing.'

14

One minute thirty. Max wondered if he would ever get used to making a living out of other people's pain. He sat there thinking about Frank Ackroyd, his old boss. 'Original sin,' Frank used to be fond of saying. 'Thank God for it, lad. It pays your bloody wages.'

'No good being a wimp in this profession,' Frank always said. 'No good tossing and turning at night about the nasty things that people do to each other, because they'll go on doing them anyway and there's sod all you or I can do about it.'

No doubt Frank was right, but Max still couldn't stand seeing Helen in this state. Fear and tension in every muscle of her body.

He sat staring at the window of the village shop, stacked with sweet jars, and attempted to shake off the heavy-headed, depressed feeling that had been hanging over him all morning.

A minute. Fifty-nine. Fifty-eight . . .

'Oh, come on . . . !' whispered Helen. She wrapped her clasped hands tightly around her knees.

'Won't be long now,' Max said, hoping to God she wasn't going to explode on him. Jump the gun. Ruin the whole thing by blazing away from the carefully prepared plan of operation . . .

Twenty-nine. Suddenly, he spotted something in the rear mirror. Here she is, Max, he told himself, right on cue. Today, the girl's dressed in red and black. Short, flared skirt and leather jacket. She's not rushing. The kids are, though . . . The boy's wearing a baseball hat, also red and black. He's nibbling at a finger of toast.

Helen clutched his arm. He felt the lightning passing through her.

'Yes?'

'Yes. That's Luke. And Leila.' First, her face was white, then it flooded with colour.

They watched the girl come out of the gate and close it behind them. No sign of Liam this morning. That's how Max wanted it.

'They're coming this way!' Helen sat there, quite frozen. Beyond her, an empty window box with geranium pots. A baker's van began its journey down the long, straggling village street.

Would the girl notice their parked car? Apparently not. Max had carefully chosen his spot, just along from the paper shop. All sorts of people parked there while they popped in for a paper.

The girl towed the children past the shop. She was almost parallel with them on the pavement. Max turned the key and started the engine. 'OK. Go for it!' he told Helen.

It went like clockwork – well, almost. As Max leapt out, he saw the wig go flying into the back seat. But Helen was out of the passenger door on the far side.

'What the . . . !' the girl screamed.

'Mummy! Mummy!' the boy cried out.

Helen pulled Luke towards her, but, for a second, the girl hung on to his other arm. Helen kicked her on the shin hard. She squealed and let go.

Max already had Leila underneath his arm. The child was crying, her mouth wide open in a silent roar. Then they were back in the car and tearing off.

'The end stall, Mrs Blair . . . It's far too close to the door. There'll be a log jam.'

Elizabeth met Margaret Fleming's gaze over the pile of quilts. She didn't intend to move the stall if she could help it. 'Well now, a lot of folk would say it's fine as it is.'

'But I'm not a lot of folk, Mrs Blair. We'll move it further back towards the window.'

After a morning spent with Margaret Fleming on her back, Elizabeth was just about ready for the men in white coats. They were preparing the lecture room for the bring-your-own-quilt afternoon and more had been brought in than, frankly, Elizabeth had expected. They were taking some arranging and Margaret's interference was making the job ten times harder.

The woman was preposterous . . . a complete obsessive . . . going on and on telling you how to do things, how Tom would like them done. She had to oversee every little detail about every goddamned thing. Fuss, fuss, fuss. Jack-rabbiting from one detail to another, until you longed to hold her down and nail her to the polished strip-pine floor.

'Come along,' Margaret said briskly. 'You take one end and I'll take the other.'

Elizabeth made one last attempt to hold her ground. 'The thing is, this exhibition was my idea. I'd kind of like to run it in my own fashion.'

'I'm sure you would, my dear, but I know what works at the Wetherburn, so if you don't mind, we'll move it.'

Two hundred years ago, Elizabeth thought, you'd have been drowned as a witch.

They moved the whole thing, lock, stock and barrel. Half-way through the proceedings, Oliver Fleming hovered into view, noted which way the wind was blowing and retreated back upstairs to his private hidey-hole.

If he was still sane after half a lifetime with Margaret, it was nothing short of a miracle.

It was half-past twelve before there was time to slope off home for lunch, but even then, Margaret followed her out along the passage to the back exit. There didn't seem to be any reason for her to be in that part of the building. She kept her own car parked at the front.

Elizabeth was fishing in her bag for her keys when Margaret's voice said, 'By the way, you didn't tell me you were involved with the Shepard Agency.'

So that was the reason for her ill temper! 'You didn't ask,' Elizabeth told her.

Margaret's jaw tightened. 'I hope you realize, Mrs Blair, that your duties here are purely as visiting lecturer? Mr Maddocks wouldn't take kindly to your poking around here for any other reason.'

'Did he say so?'

'He doesn't need to. I know how he would feel about it and I'm perfectly qualified to warn you about such activities.'

'Well, now, it's nice to know that you two are such good buddies. A man needs all the female comfort he can get at this difficult time.' In an even more sugary voice, she said, 'I'm sure your husband would agree, if I were to ask him . . .'

'And what do you mean by that?' Margaret asked.

'Oh, nothing. So long, Mrs Fleming.'

And before Margaret could say another word, Elizabeth shot off up the steps to the car-park.

Back home, she put yesterday's casserole in to warm and picked up the local paper that had been shoved through the door.

The Parish Council were examining a new road plan. Villagers were up in arms about it already. A stolen car had crashed in a high-speed chase. The Bath Minuet Company were to put on a Georgian Ball.

'Rural communities are under threat,' said the newscaster on the one o'clock bulletin. 'But the government says it doesn't have the kind of money needed to keep them ticking over.'

Next door, Dottie was watching the repeat of *Coronation Street*. She could hear the theme tune through the wall. Dottie was getting increasingly deaf. Must grab her some time, Elizabeth thought, and ask her to keep the volume down. Outside, the sky was worryingly dark. She hoped they weren't going to have a storm. Jack Hillman hadn't been to replace the missing slate on her roof.

She took a plate out of the cupboard and placed it in the oven to warm. When she'd told Hal the roof had sprung a leak, she thought he would have a fit. 'Why go buy an English hovel?' he'd asked.

'It's not a hovel. It's just that the roof hasn't been touched since 1914.'

Dottie had told her this only last week. She remembered young Herbert Emm working on the roof the day they had the telegram to say her brother was wounded in Ypres.

Impossible, however, to make Hal understand that to be without roof felting was OK over here. You could drift along without it for quite some time – eighty years or so – without too much harm being done.

I should ring him back, she told herself when she'd polished off the casserole. Let him know the place hasn't collapsed on me. Hal had been on her mind this last day or so. She felt mean about not being able to pop in on him while Hannah was in LA. He'd get miserable, he'd stuff himself with junk food and leave the cartons in the kitchen for a week. He'd talk to himself and get pie-eyed on Sunday afternoons.

Then there was Thanksgiving . . .

A minute later, she was dialling his number.

'Yeah. Who is it?'

'Hal? What kind of way is that to answer the phone?'

'What?'

'Bad-tempered. Like a bear sat on a thistle.'

'I just slammed the front door and had to let myself in again. Anyway, my foot hurts.'

'What's wrong with it?'

'Arthritis. I feel lousy.'

'What you need is a vacation. Did you think any more about coming over for Thanksgiving?'

'I thought about it.'

'And?'

'And I'm too old to come chasing across the ocean.'

'Too old? What nonsense!'

101

'It'd take too long. And anyway, I don't like the hostesses they've got nowadays.'

'What's wrong with them?'

'They're not like the old sort. They won't let you smoke a pipe. And the last plane I went on, they played tunes and I had trouble with my teeth.'

'Your teeth?'

'Got one that plays up at altitude. Gives me hell.'

'You should get it fixed.'

'I can't afford it. Know what they charge these days?'

'For heaven's sake,' Elizabeth said. 'You're so obstinate!'

'Guess it runs in the family . . .'

And she hadn't even gotten around to the roof . . .

She got out her quilting frame and began to stitch. It always soothed her. She was half-way through a Robbing Peter to Pay Paul – real bright and pretty – and it almost always gave her a good feeling.

The last one she'd worked on was a Triple Star. That had made her dizzy. You looked at it one way and you saw the stars. You looked at it another way and you saw tumbling boxes.

Almost automatically, she rethreaded her needle. Outside, the rain continued to pour down.

Your mind could wander while you stitched and it did now. Robbing Peter to Pay Paul . . . the leaking roof . . . the Wetherburn murders.

You looked at it one way and then another way . . .

And suddenly, her brain cells presented her with a connection that hadn't been there before. She sat staring at the quilt with a most peculiar expression on her face.

Margaret Fleming's temper was still variable next morning when Jane Maddocks made an unexpected visit to the office. But the weather had cleared. That was something. The sun was pouring in through the south-facing windows.

'You're not supposed to be here!' Margaret said, as Jane came through the door.

'I know.' Jane threw her a wary glance. 'But I keep thinking of all the work piling up.'

'The work can wait.' Margaret's sour gaze rested sourly on Elizabeth. 'Mrs Blair can cope with a lot of it . . . with sensible guidance.'

Elizabeth ignored her. 'I hope you don't mind me using your office,' she said to Jane.

'Not at all.' Jane looked indifferent and jaded. 'I just need a few files. I think they're in the bottom drawer.'

She drifted across to the desk and began opening and shutting drawers in the way you do when you haven't a clue where to start looking. Unwisely, Elizabeth moved out of her way and in doing so, backed into Margaret, who said abruptly, 'You may as well go and have a coffee. There isn't enough room for three of us in such confined quarters.'

'I had one half an hour back.'

'Then have another.'

Elizabeth held back the sharp retort that would have come most naturally to her in the face of such surliness. Better to hold her tongue and watch and listen.

Wasn't there something odd in the way Margaret, thin and antagonistic in her tweed jacket, thought she could coolly order around her boss's wife? Why was she standing there watching Jane like a sharp-eyed hawk? Why didn't Jane simply tell her to go fry her face?

Margaret said, 'Does Tom know you're here?'

'No.' Once more, Jane started to ferret around in the filing cabinet. She slammed the bottom drawer and opened another.

'I thought young Quennell was helping you.' Margaret came nearer. 'Is he being difficult again? Throwing temper tantrums –'

'He's not being difficult. He's at college, remember?'

'When he feels like it . . .'

Crash! A tray of paper clips crashed to the floor. Jane had caught them with her elbow.

'*Damn!*' She knelt to pick them up.

Margaret Fleming couldn't hide her irritation. 'Leave them,' she snapped. 'I'll do it later.'

Elizabeth remembered all those hens turning on each other when they were crammed into cages. She took hold of Jane's arm. 'Come and have a coffee. We'll find the files later.'

For a second, Jane seemed to be battling with her conscience. Then she gave in. 'That *would* be nice.'

Margaret's expression, as they went out through the door, changed from impatience to wariness.

OK, sure, Elizabeth thought. You think I'm up to something. Well, that suits me fine, as it happens.

There were only three people in the Tavern: Stan, the caretaker, in his navy dungarees, and a couple of oldies ensconced in the high-back settle in front of the fire.

'Quiet,' Elizabeth said.

'It always is in November.' Jane stirred sugar into her coffee.

'I haven't seen your husband around. Where does he hide himself all day?'

'Tom? He works from his desk in the flat. Says he gets more done that way. There's always something for him to see to. The Wetherburn's his life.'

'Do you ever resent that?'

'Resent it?' Jane's head came up. 'If I did, I'd have left years ago. No, I've got used to the fact that the Wetherburn comes first in his life.'

'Do you mind me asking something? Did the police get on to you? Only Max went to see Richard Nowak . . .'

Jane smiled bitterly. 'Yes. They told me that Philly was pregnant.'

'I'm so sorry. That guy's a real jerk.'

'And the father of my grandchild . . .'

'What will you do now?'

'Help her. Support her. At least he's out of her life, Mrs Blair. That's all I want. Whatever she does about the child, she'll have my backing.'

'And your husband's?' Elizabeth asked.

'Well, maybe that's different. Philly's never accepted him as a father and he finds that difficult to handle. Families are such strange things. If they don't gel, sometimes there's damn all you can do about it. Tom had a strange upbringing himself, you know. He clashed a lot with his father, so he's not likely to have a fantastic sense of family togetherness.'

'But he was close to his sister?'

'Yes, of course.'

Elizabeth looked past her. There at the coffee counter, trim and

104

neat in a camel jacket and dark trousers, stood Ruth Dando. Jane, who was sitting with her back to the counter, couldn't see her.

'They stuck to each other for comfort,' Jane said. 'Stuck like glue.'

'Glue?' Elizabeth hadn't been listening.

'Siblings do when they're having a bad time. I often wish Philly had had a brother or sister. It might have helped.'

Ruth looked round. Saw the two of them.

'But it wasn't to be. Maybe if Tom had wanted children, we'd have done something about it, but . . .'

Ruth dropped the tray she was holding back in the rack. Replaced her cookie.

'I do see what you mean,' said Elizabeth. She watched Ruth Dando, taut and angry, walk away from the counter and out through the door.

Jane was glancing at her watch. 'Is that the time? Look, I'll have to get those files. I have to be at the bank by one.'

When Elizabeth got back to the shop, the phone rang. It was Max. 'Fancy a trip into the Mendips tomorrow?' he said. 'We're going to have tea with Lampard.'

15

'So what do we do when we get there?' Elizabeth had lost her place on the map that lay folded at right angles in her lap.

'If we get there.' Max peered through the windscreen at a signpost that was half buried in the hedge. 'Temple Gurney,' he said. 'Ring any bells?'

'Sorry.' It had been a long trip through narrowing lanes. They had passed a derelict barn, a couple of cramped cottages. But there was no sign of the goat farm mentioned in Lampard's directions.

'You're useless at navigating.' Max told her.

'I know. But I've got other skills. So what did Lampard say on the phone?'

'Didn't speak to Lampard. He's clever. Led me on a real wild-goose chase last week. Meet me in Popjoy's Hotel, he said. He's not there, is he? Then the girl at the desk says there's a message. Sorry, your friend can't make it. Meet him at this place out on the Mendips instead.'

They were climbing, now, up over a bare, windswept landscape. 'And is it safe to meet him miles from anywhere?' Elizabeth asked.

'Shouldn't think so for one minute. That's why I brought you along.'

'For protection?'

'You got it.'

'Hmm. Thanks, Max.' English sense of humour, she thought. Bear with it. As an experiment, she turned the map on its side. It didn't help. 'Well, you sure couldn't get much more off the beaten track.'

Not far away, beyond the edge of the next ridge, were dry-stone walls and a low clump of trees. Above their heads, the sky was grey, but the fields shone greenish over the hard skeleton of the limestone that lay in bony streaks underneath.

'So tell me the six essential facts I should know about Lampard,' Elizabeth said.

'He's a loner. A slogger who got nowhere in the Civil Service, so looked for excitement outside. Probably took a perverse enjoyment in his hidden life. For a lot of years, his ALF activities remained untraced by any security checks.'

Max went on, 'From what I can gather, he's a tactician. All his pleasure comes from the planning of successful operations. He doesn't need to go on them. What else? He's an elusive bugger. Reckons his phones are tapped and his mail's opened before he gets it. So you can only contact him through this network of secretaries and minions. Yesterday, waiting in that hotel, it felt like being in a bad spy movie . . . comically melodramatic. But it achieves what he wants it to. You feel threatened by his absence. You almost feel like you're being sucked into his vacuum.'

They came to another crossroads, unmarked this time. The lane to the left of them petered out, fifty yards down, into a dirt track. The right turn looked like it would lead back the way they'd come. 'Straight ahead,' Elizabeth said decisively. The afternoon was getting colder.

'Want to hear one of his pamphlets?' Max asked, fiddling with the car radio.

'Hear a pamphlet?' She didn't follow.

'A tape. Andy got me a copy. They brought it back from a raid on an ALF house.' He'd found the power knob. For three seconds, the strains of a pop song from Radio 1 hollered into Elizabeth's ears. 'Sorry,' he said, noting her expression. He turned the volume down several notches and fed a tape in. 'Unknown voice. A bit spooky, actually. You won't like it.'

He couldn't have been more right. The voice – male – was cold, with a scary resonance. It sounded like something that had come in from outer space.

'Houses don't burn down by themselves. They need YOU! This so-called scientist keeps his wife and two spoiled brats in a luxurious, seven-bedroomed home in seven acres of parkland. All of it purchased with the blood of animals tortured in his laboratories! Why not let him know what you think about this? His name is Dr David Spears. He lives at The Gables, North Halling, Gloucestershire.'

Violent, paranoid, thought Elizabeth, trying not to shiver. It made your flesh chill.

'This scum will lose his life. He will get our personal attention. Adopt an animal abuser. Make his life pure hell . . .'

'Who's this trash intended for?' Elizabeth asked.

'ALF members keen enough to write letters, make anonymous calls, generally hound the unfortunate Dr Spears and his colleagues.' Max reached for the eject button. 'Heard enough?'

She certainly had. The road twisted left at the top of the hill and ran down past a no man's land covered with pale meadow herb and scattered with something that was black and glittering.

'Old lead mines,' Max said. 'They must be on the map.'

If they were, Elizabeth couldn't find them. When she got sick of looking, she dumped the map in the glove compartment and sat drinking in the view. Mile after mile of rolling hills, then violet haze, then the distant sea. It was beautiful.

'I keep seeing him in the pulpit,' Max said, 'breathing hell- fire and damnation.'

'Who? Lampard?' Elizabeth raised an eyebrow.

'His grandfather was a Welsh preacher. Lampard's found a pulpit of a different kind. He was a popular public speaker when he ran the ALF shebang in the Midlands. Drew big audiences.' His foot slammed down on the brake. 'Is that a workman's hut? That was in the directions.'

The hut stood in the ditch next to a seven-barred gate. Dirty windows, faded red canvas, leaning at an angle. Behind it, a narrow, rutted track ran into the woods.

A spotty youth in an anorak and a balaclava burst out of the hut. He was muttering into a walkie-talkie set and looked faintly ridiculous, like a train spotter indulging in para-military fantasies.

The youth yanked open the driver's door. 'Get in the back,' he said. 'Both of you. On the floor and keep your heads down.'

'On the floor?' Elizabeth said.

'Shut up. Do as you're told. And hurry.'

Play-acting, Elizabeth thought. He likes the cloak and dagger stuff. Silly young idiot. But she didn't argue.

Interminable bumping over deeply rutted tracks. Then a smoother bit, uphill. Finally, a patch of softer bumping, as if rolling down across a field.

'Get out,' the youth said, and shoved them up some rickety steps.

So here they were squashed up on vinyl seats in a stuffy caravan at the bottom of a mangy field. Now and then, Lampard stroked the Jack Russell terrier he held on his lap.

Everything was dim with the curtains half drawn. It felt claustrophobic, the three of them in there with the door and windows tight shut.

Outside, the train spotter was prowling up and down with his walkie-talkie, doing his best to look gruesome.

'Sorry about the charades,' said Lampard. 'We never used to take such measures, but we've had a lot of trouble with plain-clothes men trying to infiltrate. Can't trust the police these days, you know. It's not *Dixon of Dock Green* any more. I understand you're private detectives? So what can I do for you?'

Max said, 'We're making enquiries about the Wetherburn murders.'

'So what makes you think I can help?'

'Well, you did make violent threats against Jane Maddocks.'

'Well, now, the lady happened to make a few threats of her own.'

'Not surprising, under the circumstances, is it?'

'And what circumstances would those be?'

Lampard's voice was charming, attractive. He looked like a

slightly down-at-heel solicitor, behind an almost sinister pair of gold-rimmed glasses. His eyes were blue and piercing, there was silver in the light brown hair. He was wearing a tweed jacket and worn corduroys. He was not a big man, but he had a powerful presence that was too large for the enclosed quarters. Lampard's fingers constantly caressed the dog's ear.

'She alleges that you incited her daughter to commit acts of violence.'

He laughed. 'I'd say the young lady was quite a firebrand before I met her, wouldn't you?' His blue gaze held on to Elizabeth's and there was a provocative gleam in it as he said, 'She's a theatrical little thing.'

Max shifted the subject slightly. 'So how do you feel about using violence on ALF raids?'

'Personally speaking, I don't like it. But I wouldn't condemn anyone who used it – in a good cause. If people use violence to save animals, it's the government's fault for not bringing in legislation to wipe out factory farms.'

'So you can commit murder,' Elizabeth said, 'and blame it on your MP?'

He turned his head towards her. Waited a chilly moment and then said, 'I don't suppose you've been inside a battery shed? I worked in one for a month when I was a student. Ever seen a madhouse of hysterical hens? Ever seen one crawl under her cagemates again and again, trying not to lay? Hanging on to her egg as long as possible? All her instincts tell her she has to build a nest, see. There's an inborn reluctance to lay an egg in a crowd. Like people defecating . . .'

Elizabeth looked away, unable for the moment to meet his eyes. He had wrong-footed her, but she schooled her face to an expression of pleasant enquiry. 'You haven't answered my question. Would you countenance murder in a good cause?'

'We're back to the Wetherburn, are we?' He sighed and shook his head. 'Now that's a leading question. I don't think I'd better answer it.' Lampard glanced at them both, his eyes harder now and wary. 'What's the relationship between you two? Are you partners or what?'

'Max and I work in tandem. We're kind of useful to each other,' Elizabeth told him.

He examined the idea for a moment. 'Anybody else involved?'

'There's Caroline. She makes the tea and mans the shop.' Sweet as candy, she said, 'Anything else you want to know?'

'Not at the moment.'

The window behind his head was steaming up. As the dog started to whine, Lampard said, 'Yes, we'll go for a walk in the woods later. Yes, we will. But we have to deal with our visitors first.'

Deal with. Why did that sound so menacing?

'Good. Then perhaps we can get back down to business. Would you kill someone in order to save a few chickens?'

He shrugged. 'Sometimes it may be necessary. Accidents happen.'

'Are you saying that Joanna Drew's murder was an accident?'

'Well, now, you're putting words into my mouth.' He studied her through pale blue eyes. 'So what brings an American to our neck of the woods?'

'Oh . . . your quaint, old-fashioned way of life. Did you ever have relationships with the young girls you recruited into your organization?'

'Who told you that?' His manner was growing irritated. She guessed that he might not be able to handle losing the advantage in an argument.

'Gossip gets around. You know what it's like. I'm surprised the newspapers haven't ever picked up on it.'

'There's nothing to pick up on.' He smiled to make a joke of it, but he leaned forward as he spoke and suddenly the insistence in his voice was subtly menacing. 'You'd better be careful what you're spreading.'

'I just wondered what kind of hold you had over Philly Lucas?'

'Not that kind, I assure you.' His face was bland, his eyes dead.

I believe you, Elizabeth thought. Essentially, you're cold-blooded. You wouldn't want to lose control . . .

'Then I guess we'll have to try another tack. How would you have felt if Jane Maddocks had died instead of her sister-in-law?'

'I can't honestly say I would have lost sleep.' Suddenly, there was a chilling purity in his voice. And the way he looked at you . . . Oh, yes, Elizabeth thought. You're the kind who would brood and brood and then lash out. If you set out to kill someone, you'd have a foolproof plan.

110

He was the planner. The ex-taxman. Used to counting and accounting for every little detail.

Max said, 'Did you ever meet Joanna Drew?'

'Once, briefly. She came marching into my office about six weeks ago. Stormed past my secretary and gave me a lecture about making her sister-in-law's life hell.'

'That's interesting.'

'I'd choose a different word. If you ask me, the woman was unhinged.'

'At any rate, you'd know Mrs Drew on sight?'

'Oh, yes. But you wouldn't have much of a case if you tried to prove that I killed her. Or Jane Maddocks, for that matter. I was in South Wales that night.'

'I bet he wasn't.' Elizabeth said, nodding her head towards the window and the train spotter.

'Who? Lee? Don't make me laugh.'

'I must admit he doesn't seem too bright a specimen. But there are plenty more little yobbos who'd only be too happy. Your friends who fired Reuben's place, for instance. You didn't happen to send them up to fire the Wetherburn shop, by any chance?'

'Would I be that stupid, with the police already on my back?' Lampard leaned forward, his lips curling into that so mocking smile. 'Listen – there are plenty of other people who disliked Mrs Drew enough to want to, shall we say, silence her.'

'Such as?'

'Well, let's see now. So many skeletons in so many cupboards. Where do I start?'

'With the most obvious?' Elizabeth suggested.

He smiled unpleasantly.

'Who was most scared of Mrs Drew?'

He was enjoying himself. 'The Flemings, I should think Margaret and Oliver. Joanna Drew knew things about them that could lose Oliver his job.'

Elizabeth said, 'Would you mind telling me how you know that?'

Lampard laughed. 'It came from little Philly. Well, indirectly.'

'What does that mean?'

'Philly told Rick. Pillow talk, my dear. You can learn all sorts of things that way, they tell me.'

111

'And Nowak told you?'

'Well, I'm not a mind-reader.' His voice was heavy with sarcasm. He was a clever so-and-so . . .

'And how did Philly get to know about it?'

'Apparently, she overheard a certain conversation between Mrs Drew and the publicity lady. Mrs Drew said she knew something about Oliver's past that Tom wouldn't care for. She seemed to be threatening them . . .'

'Philly didn't mention it to me,' Max said.

'Well, perhaps you didn't ask the right questions. Or perhaps little Miss Lucas ran rings about you.' It wouldn't be difficult, his gaze implied.

Boy, was he a sleazeball. When he hit you, he didn't leave a mark. 'Did you mention this to the police?'

'Why should I help them solve their case?' Lampard said. 'Or yours, for that matter.' He looked straight at Elizabeth. 'You're wasting my valuable time. So I'd be most grateful if you'd leave my property and stay off it in future.'

It was good to get out into the fresh air. Out into the woods and the wind. The thing Elizabeth remembered most was the chilly gaze behind Lampard's blue-eyed smile.

'Bumptious,' said Max.

'Thinks the law doesn't apply to him.' Elizabeth could imagine him itching to get even with Jane and Philly. Unable to rest until he'd done so. You could smell it on him.

At last, they were bumping down the lane that led to the main road. A pheasant ran across in front of them. Beautiful plumage, hopping along like mad. In another minute, it would be gone.

It was as they turned the corner that something struck the windscreen. Fractured the glass up in one corner, making Max swerve.

'What the hell?'

Something else hit the dusty road in front of them. Max put his foot down on the accelerator.

'Somebody shot at us!' Elizabeth said when they reached the safety of the main road.

'I don't think so.'

'Max – it hit us! I saw it.'

'What you saw was a stone from a catapult,' Max said. 'Classic ALF weapon. Good for shattering shop windows. Probably that moron with the balaclava. Let's get out of here.'

16

Elizabeth checked out the shop when they got back into town and found Caroline with her head deep in a book. It had been frantic from eleven to twelve, but after that, business had died. May as well go home then, Elizabeth thought. But then she remembered Joanna Drew's funeral service. Two o'clock, at St Swithin's. If she hurried, she'd just catch them as they came out.

It was just after three when she parked under the church wall and sat, quietly watching the mourners spill out through the lych-gate.

It wasn't a good weather afternoon. Dark sky, no wind. Sodden leaves in compressed layers under the churchyard wall. On such days, these English villages could feel oppressive. There were moments (only occasional) when Elizabeth wished herself back in the wild and open spaces where you could see the wild turkey fly.

But it was a kind of comfort that here, in the village of South Harptree, everyone went to everyone else's funeral. There was an odd security in knowing precisely who had died and when and where. Even in death, you were assured of attention.

The undertaker, a stocky man with grizzled hair, climbed back into his limousine. Tom Maddocks, eyes red-rimmed, emerged from the crowd, accepting sincerely offered sympathy in a daze, as if he'd forgotten who he was and what he was doing there.

Jane stood by his side in dark grey. She looked exhausted. At last, she took his arm and steered him towards their car.

A sharp burst of rain. More mourners. The corpse, trapped in a fine oak coffin, lay waiting for the final stage of the journey, to the crematorium.

The crowd was thinning as Reuben Dando, awkward and bulky and ungainly, crossed the road by the pub. And there was Ruth, stony-faced by his side.

And Nick Quennell, his coat collar turned up against the rain.

Quennell wasn't alone. The solitary-looking young man in a leather jacket next to him would be Tim. Same height, same sandy features. All sorts of emotions shut up in his thin, young face.

Tom and Jane were only yards away, standing by the limousine, but Quennell Senior seemed to move in a wide semicircle to avoid speaking to them. Almost as if they'd had some difference of opinion. Now that was interesting.

The funeral party slowly set off. The Quennells were coming her way. Elizabeth bided her time, then wound down the window. 'Want a lift?' she asked. 'Or did you drive up?'

Quennell hesitated. 'I've got my car. But you could drop Tim off, if you like. I've got to go into town and it would save me a detour.'

'Jump right in. No problem.' She threw Tim Quennell a beaming smile. 'We haven't met. I'm Elizabeth Blair. I've taken over Jane's lectures at the Wetherburn.'

'Oh. Right. Sure you don't mind?' Tim said, as they drove out of the village.

'Not at all. How's your mother?'

'Not too good. That's why I'm home. We had an intruder at the cottage. I think the shock set her back.'

'It would. Did they take anything?'

'Not that we can tell. They just made a hell of a mess. Luckily they didn't get down to Mum's room.'

Elizabeth gave the boy a quick, sideways glance as they set off up Rectory Hill. 'Look – I'm not sure if you've heard, but I also work with my friend, Max, of the Shepard Detective Agency. Would you mind if I asked about your relationship with Jane Maddocks?'

Tim turned his head, startled. He said abruptly, 'I don't have a relationship with Jane.'

'You didn't have a crush on her?'

'Who told you that?' He had flushed.

'Let's just say an impeccable source.' Or a blind guess.

'My father . . .' Tim's expression was a wonderful mixture of cynicism and disgust. 'Bastard!' he muttered under his breath.

'No.' Elizabeth threw him another glance as they approached the junction. 'Margaret Fleming mentioned tension between you and

114

Jane. That's why I'm asking. I don't suppose you'd care to tell me about it?'

'No, I bloody well wouldn't! I'll get out here, if you don't mind. I'd rather walk home than answer any of your stupid questions.'

Elizabeth paused momentarily at the halt sign and, seeing an empty road, accelerated before he could reach the door handle. 'I expect you would. But I'll be easier on you than the police would. Look, Tim, I'm on your side. And if you have nothing to hide, then there's no need to worry.'

He sat there, staring stubbornly ahead of him. Giving his predicament silent, brooding consideration.

'Why were you mad with Jane? What caused the friction?'

'It was nothing. I was just being stupid. There was something I couldn't handle at the time.'

'Like your father's friendship with Jane Maddocks?'

'How did you know that?'

'I have children.' She threw him a glance and chanced a guess. 'You were jealous. Was that it?'

Silence.

'Tim?'

His face was in a panic. 'Look, it was a whole age ago. I spent the summer working with Jane and I thought I was in love with her. It was just one of those physical things that build up. Anyway, one night, in her office, I made a pass at her and she put me in my place. I resented it and I exploded at her. I made a complete fool of myself.'

'And now you regret it?'

'Too right,' he said blackly.

'I don't suppose you'd like to tell me about the relationship between your father and Mrs Maddocks?'

Was that fear lurking at the back of his eyes, behind the sullenness? 'You'll have to ask him about that. I don't live here any more.'

'One more thing. What were you doing on the night Joanna Drew was killed?'

'I was in town visiting a friend.'

Well within reach, Elizabeth thought, if you had enough hate and jealousy boiling up inside of you.

She dropped him at the cottage. 'Thanks for the lift,' he said.

'Thanks for talking to me,' Elizabeth replied, ignoring the sarcasm in his voice. He'd get out of the way fast next time he saw her coming. She would bet her last dollar on that.

Fine cloud drifted down over the woods and the valley. There were lights on the top floor of the Wetherburn, up on the hill. Shadowy scaffolding stood silhouetted against the sky on the west wing.

The gates were standing open as she drove past. She could see the tall Georgian windows rising above the trees. It was a splendid old house . . . one of the finest for miles. Floors beeswaxed by half a dozen maids in the old man's time, Dottie had said.

Imagine cleaning all those floors by hand . . .

Her own cottage was easier to maintain, thank goodness. Small and cosy enough to cook and eat and watch TV at the same time. Shelves crammed with books and baskets of patchwork made the place seem even more nest-like.

Taking off her raincoat, she poked up the wood-burning stove and went into the kitchen to put the kettle on. She was about to start toasting teacakes, when the phone rang.

'Hi! It's Max. I'm off into Bristol. I've persuaded Helen to eat out with me at a tapas bar. Er . . . I don't suppose you'd like to join us?'

'It's a kind thought, Max. But I'd cramp your style.'

'No. Really.'

'Listen, I appreciate the offer, but I'm whacked. You go ahead and enjoy yourself. By the way, how are her children?'

'Unsettled, but they'll be OK. I'm more worried about Helen. She's a bag of nerves. Keeps expecting her husband to leap out of every passing car. I've persuaded her to stay at my place for a few days.'

'Is that wise? Max – there's a golden rule in your business.'

'Yeah, yeah. Don't get involved. Well, it's a bit late for that.'

'Oh, Max – while you're there . . . do me a favour.'

'What's that?'

'Get your policeman friend, Andy, to check Tom Maddocks' financial state for me.'

'I can tell you that for nothing. He's loaded.'

'I'd just like to make sure of that.'

'OK. I'll see you tomorrow.'

Elizabeth put the receiver down and sighed. She knew what Max was like with women, but it was useless to interfere. She went back to the kitchen to make the tea.

Which was fatal, because it always brought Dottie around and today was no exception. 'How are you?' Elizabeth asked her, when she appeared on the doorstep two minutes later.

'Feeling like two halfpence worth of nothing,' Dottie replied.

Whatever that meant . . . Still, it was probably nothing that a cup of tea wouldn't cure.

'Your dahlias look unhappy,' Dottie told her, as soon as she'd ensconced herself next to the fire.

They might be having full-scale nervous breakdowns, Elizabeth thought. I wouldn't know.

'Still, they're resilient things, dahlias. You can mistreat them as much as you like. They'll still come back for more.' A pause. 'Like some people,' she added.

Elizabeth thought of Oliver Fleming and was inclined to agree.

'I don't spray,' Dottie said. 'Do you?'

'Dahlias?'

'What else, dear?'

'No,' said Elizabeth. 'No, I don't.'

'Only I've just written a long letter to the *Chronicle* on the subject.' Dottie concentrated on buttering her teacake and dividing it into four neat quarters, which she proceeded to pick the currants out of. Suddenly, she said, 'I've been wondering if you'd like a little trip out to the theatre some time? I find these long winter nights rather tiresome.'

Elizabeth made semi-agreeable noises.

'In the old days, we used to go up to London to see Ivor Novello. Edmund – my brother, you know – was a Turk about punctuality. Once, he got us there so early, we were standing around in evening dress in broad daylight . . .'

Somewhere in the junk-room of Elizabeth's mind, something stirred. A picture. A snatch of conversation . . . On her own again, she sat there rummaging around in her memory for what it was that Dottie had reminded her of.

The fire was going down. She reached for a log with a frown on her forehead. After a moment's thought, her face cleared. Yes, she knew what it was. What she ought to check on . . .

117

It was blowing a gale and raining at nine that evening, when she went to put the garbage out. The wrought-iron light by the back door was rocking in the wind.

'Bleak,' she told herself, shoving the bolt over hard. The kind of night to curl up in front of a good film. Which made her think, suddenly, for no reason at all, of the training video that Laura Eyton had made. The one that Margaret Fleming had reluctantly handed over.

She dug it out of the cupboard and slotted it into the machine. Laura was standing in the Quilt Room, looking for all the world as if she owned the place. Her hair tinted a delicate shade of hazel, her head tilted so as to show off her best profile. Behind her, sunlight on the panelling. Must have been last summer . . .

Laura was saying, 'You are here to give information to the visitors and to answer their questions, but you are also here to keep an eye on the contents of the Wetherburn. Small objects go missing more often than you would think. We had one case of a young man with his sketchbook and rucksack –'

Was that a faint noise outside in the dark garden?

Elizabeth reached for the controller and flicked off the sound, caught by a fleeting sensation that she was not alone in the place. She sat there and listened.

There was a kind of silence, like an echo. Then the sound of rain tap-tapping on the panes.

Laura was now in close-up, mouthing words to the camera. Her eyes didn't look normal. They were too intense to go with the smile on her glossy mouth. She was enjoying herself, though, swanning around in front of the camera.

Elizabeth made herself relax and put the sound back on. 'We are not running a Leisure Centre,' Laura said. 'Swimming in the lake is strictly forbidden. As are smoking and eating in any part of the museum except the restaurant. So you must pounce on anyone who –'

Leisure Centre . . . Something went click in Elizabeth's head. That was it! That was where she had seen . . .

Click! This time it wasn't in her head, but outside the window. It was definitely audible. There was someone out there, and it wasn't the wind. Elizabeth flicked off the video. Picked up the poker that lay beside her on the hearth.

Someone was sneaking down by the side of the house. There was a lurchy feeling in the pit of her stomach.

She wanted to fling the front door open, but that would be stupid. Better to turn the lamp off and peer out.

The room now glowed in the bluish light of the television. She stayed where she was for a long time, then tiptoed to the window. Another minute and she would have lifted the curtain.

But suddenly the door bell rang.

A tall shadow stood in the doorway against the porch light. Then it spoke. 'What the hell kind of place is this that doesn't have street-lamps?'

'Hal!' She almost collapsed against him in relief.

17

'How am I supposed to have a bath in this thimble-shaped thing?' Hal hollered down the stairs. Twice, the night before, he had hit his head on a beam and he was too tall to lie straight in the spare bed.

'Take a shower,' Elizabeth yelled back as she emptied the bowl of water she had collected from the roof. But at least it had stopped raining. In the night, the wind had turned. Now there was an icy feel to the air.

'You should hassle that builder,' Hal said when he appeared at the breakfast table. He hadn't changed one bit since she saw him last. He had more silver in his hair, but wore the same hangdog expression, had the same slouching walk. He gave the impression that nothing short of an earthquake would cause him to change speed.

'I rang him three times last week. He's got bigger fish to fry. Chiefly, the Wetherburn roof. But I'm going on over there later to have a go at him.'

Hal helped himself to cornflakes. 'Why the hell did you buy such a run-down, beat-up old place?'

'The English like run-down. They find it comfortable.'

'Sounds dumb to me.'

'You get used to it. So . . . what have you been doing with your-self while Hannah's away?'

Hal reached for the milk jug. 'I haven't been sleeping with strange women, if that's what you mean.'

Elizabeth gave a hoot of laughter. I've missed you, she thought.

'You're looking skinny,' Hal mumbled through his first spoonful of cornflakes. 'Need feeding up.'

It was comfortable having your brother fuss over you, though she didn't agree with his comment. 'Different eating pattern. I feel very fit. So did you see my son lately? How is he?'

'OK, I guess.'

'Now, Hal, tell the truth.'

'Well, the boy's a worrier. A real old woman.'

'Always has been. He was born that way.' Now where had that come from? Not the Lightfoot side. 'What's it this time?'

'He's losing his hair at the front. And he doesn't know if he wants a new car. Oh, and he took the air-conditioning apart and can't get it together again.'

That was Jim Junior. She buttered some more toast. 'And did you see Kate?'

Kate, Elizabeth's daughter, worked for a publisher in New York and was as crisp and down-to-earth as Jim Junior was jumpy. Jim would worry behind your back how to solve problems you never knew you had in the first place. He was a dear boy, but he tired you out. Kate shot straight from the hip, but Elizabeth rather liked that. You knew where you stood with her.

'She came down for the weekend and cooked for me.'

'Oh, dear.'

'Yeah. She's a great kid, but she talks better than she cooks.'

Now that, Elizabeth thought, *did* come from the Lightfoot side.

Hal was stirring his coffee, round and round. He suddenly changed the subject. 'You making money in that shop of yours?'

'Some.' She didn't want to talk finances at this hour of the morning.

'Not a fortune then?'

'No. But neither am I as poor as Job's turkey . . .' Which reminded her. 'Thanksgiving dinner. We'll go order something this morning.' A picture of Lampard flashed into her brain. 'Something free-range,' she said firmly. 'And while we're in town, I'll show you Martha Washington.'

Nick Quennell's cottage was trapped among trees in the valley bottom. There was a deserted, empty lane at the front. At three in the afternoon – dammit, at any time of the day – it was as silent as the grave. A cold dusk hovered over the fields and woods. In a couple of hours, there would be ice on the water in the ditch. The air was keen, invigorating and somehow ominous.

She had left Hal mooching around the bookshops in town. Had promised to pick him up from the shop later. Caroline was there to make him a pot of tea.

There was a light on in the sitting-room at the front of the cottage. After latching the gate soundlessly behind her, Elizabeth followed the crazy paving path to the stone porch and rang the bell. On the ledge to one side of the porch stood a row of upturned flowerpots and a note that said, *Knock hard. Bell doesn't work.*

The lion's head knocker made a heavy thumping sound that would waken the dead. Tim Quennell opened the door.

'It's me again,' said Elizabeth. 'Is your father in?'

'He is, but he's . . . busy.' Sullenly, he stood looking at her.

'I'd really like to talk to him, if he could spare a minute.'

A short silence. Then he said, 'You'd better come in.'

She stepped into the narrow hall. There was a fire burning in the sitting-room to the right and, out through the back door, she could see a lower garden. The smell of Dettol pervaded the atmosphere. It was like walking into a cottage hospital.

Tim shut the door on the cold. 'I'll see if I can find him.'

'Thanks. But first . . . well, I didn't get a chance to ask you yesterday. You didn't see anything suspicious down here on the night Mrs Drew was murdered? Only you live almost opposite . . .'

'I've already told the police. There was a car parked outside her house in the evening, briefly, but that's all I saw.'

'No driver?'

'It was dark. I thought I saw a woman coming down the path, but I might have been mistaken.'

'What time would this be?'

'Not sure. Eight-ish? When I got back from town.'

121

He left her standing there while he went off to find Nick. Elizabeth stood looking around. The stairs were narrow, the walls pink-washed. From a room somewhere in the back came muffled voices. A minute went by, then another. She could hear the sound of an argument going on in what was, presumably, the kitchen.

Impossible to resist the temptation.

She crept to the end of the hall and stood listening.

Tim was saying, 'Have you been giving her that stuff again?'

'What stuff?'

'You know what! I warned you –'

'Oh, for God's sake –'

'No, for Mum's sake. You don't care, do you? You don't give a damn!'

Nick's voice mumbled something.

'I don't care about you. Only her. And I'll be watching from now on . . .'

Elizabeth nipped smartly back to where Tim had left her and pretended to be deep in thought. Not a moment too soon, for, when she turned, she saw Nick Quennell in the doorway. 'Mrs Blair! This is an unexpected pleasure.'

'I hope you don't mind me dropping by?'

He came up the steps, closing the door behind him. 'Is there some kind of problem?'

'I'm just checking on a few things.' He's uneasy, she thought. He's trying to hide it, but he's not being very successful.

'You'd better come in here,' he said.

The room into which he showed her was fitted out like a study, with rows of deep bookshelves, a couple of armchairs and a desk at the far end. He put on the lamp. 'Take a seat. Will you have a drink?' he said, opening a small cupboard that stood in the corner.

'No. Thank you. But don't let me stop you.'

He poured himself a whisky. 'Don't usually indulge at this hour,' he said. 'Got a cold coming. I can feel it in my throat.'

He certainly didn't look well. There were rings under his eyes and the lids were puffy.

'Did Tim tell you we had a chat?'

'Yes. Yes, he did. How long have you been working with Max Shepard? I should have thought you had your hands full with the shop.'

122

'I've got a girl who keeps things ticking over. And I guess the long and the short of it is that I like sticking my nose in other people's business. It's the only thing, besides patchwork, that I was ever good at.' She looked him straight in the eye. 'You know, I'm amazed that you aren't mad at me for questioning your son. I half expected you to throw me out of the house. That would be the natural reaction.'

'Depends what you call natural. People react differently.'

'That's true. I just had you down as someone who would jump to protect his family when they're asked awkward and impertinent questions.' She kept her gaze on his, waiting for his answer.

'If there's one thing I've learned in life, it's that you don't explode every time you feel like it. And I've had plenty of practice at fielding awkward questions about my private life.'

'I suppose you have,' Elizabeth said. Yet somehow she was not convinced by his excuses. He was remarkably unfazed. Too unfazed. 'Tim seemed very edgy about your friendship with Jane Maddocks.'

'I don't know what you mean,' Nick said. He swallowed down half his whisky at a gulp. 'Are you sure I can't get you anything? Tea? A coffee?'

Elizabeth shook her head. In an enquiring tone, she said, 'I was thinking the other day . . . Jane has quite an effect on her male colleagues at the Wetherburn. Oliver Fleming. Tim. And Reuben Dando. Of course, I know it doesn't necessarily mean that you feel a sexual attraction towards her, but then again, it might be odd if you didn't.'

He looked a trifle shocked. 'I've never thought of her like that. I've got too much on my plate.'

'Your wife's illness. Well, if you don't mind my saying so, that would only make you more susceptible. The loneliness, the lack of a sexual partner.'

'It's incredible how these myths get around! Your wife's incapacitated, so you're expected to be bonking around with every woman in the area. Honestly, it's ludicrous!'

Elizabeth wasn't taken in by his mock jocularity. And she didn't miss the flash of panic behind his eyes. Where's the exit? they were saying. Let me get out of here – and fast!

But then he got a grip on himself. 'Look – I'll admit that Tim had a thing about Jane . . . a teenage crush. That kind of obsessive passion comes when you're askew, off-balance. He was agonized about Lucy.'

'You didn't answer my question. Did *you* find Jane Maddocks physically attractive?'

'You don't give up, do you? I'm at a loss to know what else to say. Of course she's an attractive woman, but I can't imagine why you should think I'm – what? – having an affair with her.'

'Because I saw you. That's why.'

That hit him hard in the solar plexus. His eyes almost popped out of his head with the shock. 'I beg your pardon!'

'I said I saw you – in the coffee lounge of the Links Hotel, about three months ago. It's a hotel and leisure complex near Cheltenham. I was up there delivering some quilts.'

He swallowed the rest of his whisky fast. 'You must be mistaken.'

'No. I made sure of that. I went and checked the register for August. You booked a double room under your name. That was careless.'

The shadow of an incredulous smile crossed his face. 'You're making it up to try and trick me. I've never been to the place.'

Patience is an awesome weapon. That and the knowledge that all you have to do is sit there and look at him to wear him down. He fiddled around with his glass for a bit, then got up to stride around the room. In an offhand way, he put the glass down on the table.

At last he turned. 'OK, so I did take a woman up to the Links. I'm only human, but I'm not proud of the fact that I gave in to my baser needs.' His hands were in his pockets now and he was seemingly anxious to be honest with her. His face was pale. 'It was just a one-night stand,' he insisted. 'I never saw her again. Didn't want to.' He spoke with a quiet, contained vehemence. But his eyes still wouldn't meet hers, and she knew he was still lying.

Elizabeth wouldn't let him off the hook. 'That first night when we met at the Cheese and Wine do, I knew I'd seen you before. But it didn't come back to me until yesterday. I might forget a location, but never a face. It was Jane that you were with. The receptionist recognized her photograph.'

'She might have seen her in the newspapers.'

'No. She remembered you as a couple. And Jane paid the bill.'

Silence. His shoulders seemed to slump.

'No more games. I need the truth.'

He said, 'All right. I had a brief affair with Jane Maddocks.'

18

Elizabeth relaxed a little. You can afford to be gentler now, she thought. The carrot instead of the stick. 'You told me she was kind to you. Is that where it started?'

Quennell nervously twisted the wedding ring on his finger. 'We were just friends at first. Then one night, we were on our way back from a business trip to Harrogate and the car broke down. We had to put up at a hotel. And that night . . . I can't explain it . . . but something sparked between us. We had a long dinner . . . a lovely evening.'

Elizabeth sat listening.

'I remember that she'd had a row with Tom . . .'

'What about?'

'Can't remember. She got fed up because he spent so much time and effort on the Wetherburn. Reckoned she was only part of the damned fittings. They'd been going through a bad patch, mostly caused by Philly.'

Outside, in the garden, Tim Quennell was feeding the birds with bacon scraps. He looked anxious and blue-faced in the wind. Every now and then, he would cast a glance in their direction.

'Lucy likes to watch the birds,' Nick explained. 'It's one of the few pleasures she has left. Tim always feeds them for her when he's home.'

Elizabeth waited for him to continue. Sad though his wife's illness was, she wasn't going to let him divert the course of his narrative.

'When the affair began . . . well, it was like the first day of the summer holidays when you were a child. I couldn't believe what was happening. It wasn't just the sex. We used to talk for hours and I'm not all that good at talking, especially about my feelings. I always fended people off if they got too personal. But Jane got through the barrier. She'd tease me out of my morose moods. It was healing, reviving. Suddenly, I found I could dream again. We wanted each other and to hell with the consequences. I suppose it was dangerous, but it was like gambling. Once you'd started, you couldn't stop. It was the happiest time of my entire life. No, the summer I met Lucy was the happiest. But this came close. I even found myself switching on Radio 2 in the mornings, listening to love songs. I caught Tim looking at me one morning.'

'Did he guess?'

'Not at first. I told him the song used to be Lucy's favourite when we were engaged. What could be more despicable than lying to the boy like that? But that's what happens when you're in love. You lie to cover up. Your moral principles are the first thing to go out of the window.'

Elizabeth said nothing.

'We used to be real mates, you know, when Tim was little. Sad when you lose touch with your own flesh and blood. My own fault. I should have been able to do something to break through the barrier.' He kept his eyes fixed on the bare garden. 'I couldn't tell him what was going on. What would he think? I felt torn in half.'

'Is the affair still going on?'

'Of course not. These things never last. Oh, she said she was going to leave Tom. But then I started to come to my senses. I couldn't walk out on Lucy. I told Jane it had to stop. That was when she almost decided she had to leave Tom. Make a fresh start somewhere. Her marriage was stale, she said. And it would be awkward for us both if she stayed.'

'Could she support herself?'

'No problem. Her books are selling well. And she does a lot of freelance work. Lecturing and writing for magazines here and in the States.'

'Did Joanna know about the affair?'

'There was no way she could have known. We were very careful. Believe me, Joanna would have said plenty if she *had* found out!'

She had the feeling that he was telling the truth. His face had the clear, drained look of a child who had finished owning up. In any case, she couldn't imagine him as a killer. His features expressed too much pain and sensitivity.

'And Tom?'

'He didn't know . . . I'm certain.'

'Was there anyone else who might have found out about it?'

'Philly did. I regret that, because until then, Jane and Philly seemed to be getting closer. But that blew it all apart again. Philly was very fond of Lucy, you see. She saw it as a betrayal. She was full of contempt.'

'So what did she do?'

'She told Tim, for a start. God, he was scathing. Life's all black and white to the young, isn't it? He hasn't yet learned that there are all shades of grey.' He saw Elizabeth's expression. 'But neither of those kids would have tried to kill Jane. Don't even think it. They wouldn't, that's all.'

By the time she left the cottage, it was three almost four thirty. Early twilight.

There was this screen inside her head on to which pictures were being projected. She saw Jane murdering Joanna, who was threatening to expose her affair with Nick. But that was ridiculous. These days, people just walked out of marriages they were tired of. There was no need for violence of that sort.

She saw Tom shooting his wife in a fit of mad jealousy. Hitting Joanna instead, because she was wearing that damned scarf. But he would have recognized his own sister, no matter what she had been wearing.

Next, there was Tom trying to kill his wife and Joanna trying to stop him and getting in the way of the bullets. But Jane would have told the police, surely? After all, she'd been tough enough to grass on her own daughter.

Then Nick, his nerves on a knife edge, shooting Jane because, maybe, she had called off the affair.

Tim Quennell . . . Philly . . .

The list was endless. What a hornets' nest it all was.

Max forced himself to concentrate on what Helen was saying, but it wasn't easy. She was unlike any other girl he'd ever met. Her eyes. Those deep amber flecks. And that way she had of gazing at you through them. Like she was waiting for some sort of response from you and you'd better make it quick, or else she'd turn her gaze on some other bloke fastish.

They were washing up together after dinner. The children were playing in the other room.

'. . . do you think it would?' she was asking.

'Sorry?'

'I said, do you think we should move house permanently? I mean, I don't want to, but I just don't feel safe there any more.'

'I think,' he said, 'you should take your time making decisions like that. There's no hurry. You can stay here as long as you like.'

'You're so sweet. Did I ever tell you? It makes such a difference, being with a man you can trust.' Her gaze locked into his. She wasn't smiling. 'You have no idea how much.'

'Tell me sometime.'

'Oh, I will.'

He continued to look at her. His pulse quickened.

'Max?'

'Mmm.'

'I feel quite different about life now. I want you to know that. I'd lost hope, but now . . .'

'Now . . .?'

'I almost feel I can start living again. Does that sound stupid?'

'Nothing you say sounds stupid.' He lifted a hand to touch her face. 'I'm just glad you feel safe with me.'

She stood there, smiling up at him. 'Well, not that safe, actually,' she whispered as her hand slid up his back.

His eyes moved to her lips. Her mouth was luscious; soft and curved and absolutely luscious. He kissed it gently. Then dizzily. For a few seconds in that small, cluttered kitchen, the universe stopped spinning.

'Sometimes we use the Rectory kitchen and sometimes Tithebarn. The Rectory more, lately, since Tithebarn's been under siege. Our bookings have fallen off a bit since the mock adverts in the *Chronicle*.'

Katharine Ellerton spoke with her usual sharpness, while seeing to the drinks. The Rectory drawing-room was big and draughty. It had that peculiar English country house mixture of fleabag and grandeur. There was a cheerful fire in the great hearth, but it didn't reach past the coffee table that was planted in front of it.

'And then they sabotaged Ruthie's car, so we had to use my old contraption for a while.' She turned to Reuben Dando. 'Saw your letter about the police in the *Chronicle*. Jolly brave of you to have a bash at them.'

Reuben helped himself to peanuts from the side table. 'Won't do any good. But it needed saying. They're too busy towing away cars and chasing travellers to catch ALF vermin and arsonists.'

'Oh, absolutely! I must admit they've gone too far this time. Still, Simon and I were saying last night that some of these youngsters are quite brave. The hunt saboteurs, for instance. We used to go on anti-vivi marches when we were students, didn't we, darling?'

'This is going to be fun,' Elizabeth muttered to Hal. She had rung the Ellertons to try and duck out of the dinner party, but Katharine wouldn't hear of it. Bring your brother along, she'd said. The more the merrier!

'Nothing wrong with hunting,' Reuben growled. 'Clears the vermin. Good, healthy exercise.'

'And don't some of us need it?' Ruth Dando said, with her eye on his beer belly. She had been taking not-so-discreet verbal swipes at Reuben ever since their arrival. Barbed remarks designed to wave the red flag at the bull.

'They'd ban everything if they had their way.' Reuben lumbered on regardless. 'Shooting . . . fishing. Used to love a day's shooting with old man Maddocks in the old days.'

His wife threw him a sour glance.

'I'm sorry, Reuben, but I can't endorse violence of any sort,' Katharine said. 'Got to stick to my principles. Don't you agree, Simon?'

Simon Ellerton hesitated and then decided that discretion was the better part of valour. 'In a manner of speaking. Is this your first trip to the UK, Mr . . . er . . . Blair?'

'Because if you don't stick to what you believe in, this country doesn't stand a chance.' Katharine looked around for someone to agree with her.

'Lightfoot. The name's Lightfoot.' Hal's eyes ran bemusedly around the room. They took in the the dog sleeping wheezily in the fireplace, the window seats the size of tombstones. 'Elizabeth's my sister – not my wife.'

'I'm so sorry. My perception was –'.

'Simon's hopeless with names,' Katharine said. 'Sometimes I despair.'

'Thank God,' said Hal.

'I beg your pardon?'

'Thank God she's not my wife. Let me tell you, I wouldn't care for that.'

It was Oliver Fleming who laughed, from the other side of the room. 'You'll suffer for that when you get home.'

In due course, they trooped into the dining-room, which was refined, intellectually, but smelled of dogs. There was taped Vivaldi and heavy, Georgian silver, inherited from Simon's grandmother. Katharine had prepared mackerel pâté, cheese pie and a choice of fruit compote or bread and butter pudding. They were veggies, she explained, though she did prepare the dreaded meat for business purposes. There was a plentiful supply of cheap plonk, which served to make Ruth's manner bolder and even more aggressive. Reuben, on the other hand, sat at the far end of the table, brooding silently over his glass. And as for Oliver . . . well, Oliver turned into rather a nice potato-head when he was intoxicated. He kept diving into rambling reminiscences about his schooldays and the more he rabbited on, the more officious Margaret became. Elizabeth sat there enjoying Hal's bemusement and glimpsing far more than any of them realized.

'Now, before we begin,' Katharine had said, 'anyone who mentions the Wetherburn will be immediately slung out. It's just too gruesome while we're eating.'

So they discussed, instead, the size of the Rectory. As she served the cheese pie, Katharine had a good grouse. 'Ten bedrooms! I mean, what is one supposed to do with them? Simon suggested taking in the homeless, but, honestly, one has to be practical. I said to him, Simon, if I have to cook for a dozen or more, I can't run the business. And if I don't run the business, we can't afford to pay the gas and electricity. Simple as that. The thing is, even Christians have to have a smidgeon of practicality.'

Simon gave her an uneasy look, but Katharine ploughed right on. 'Simon's got a rich aunt, so we're hoping. Not that she'll pop off immediately, of course. But if we can get her to cough up for James's school fees next year, it'll be a boon. Letty can go to the local Comp – she's not an intellectual, I'm afraid.'

'I went to school all over the place,' said Ruth, her eyes sparkling, her cheeks highly coloured. 'My father was a professional soldier, moving all the time. I was always in a state about starting a new school, but my mother said it was character-forming. She put my father first, no matter what.'

'If they had to move, they had to move,' Reuben said. 'You'd get yourself into a state about anything.'

'I used to get train-sick on the way back to school.' This contribution came from Oliver at the other end of the table. 'Never at any other time. Psychological, I suppose. I hated saying goodbye to my mother for ten weeks.'

Margaret's chair creaked as she leaned forward for the salt. She shook it sharply on to the side of her plate, but nothing at all came out. 'I think it's empty,' she said, shaking it hard.

'Just damp,' said Katharine. 'Take the top off.'

'But it was wonderful coming back at the end of term,' Oliver mused thickly. 'Never got train-sick then. I remember her waiting there on the dusty platform. She counted the days until my return. A widow, you see. Missed me no end.'

Margaret rapped the salt cellar hard on the table. It was clear she was getting furious with it. Or with Oliver. 'So how did you finish up in South Harptree?' she asked Ruth.

'We came here on holiday when I was eighteen.'

'And you fell in love with Reuben?' Katharine was egging her on. There could be no doubt.

'I suppose I must have done.' Ruth gulped down the wine in her glass.

'Don't tell me. He was tall, dark and handsome and he set your pulses racing.'

'Something like that.' Ruth held out her glass to Simon, who was going around with the bottle. 'I also fell in love with Tithebarn, would you believe? With the old farmhouse and the orchards and the scent of the hay meadows . . .'

Reuben's face darkened.

'Hay meadows?' Katharine said. 'Goodness, things have changed!'

'Certainly have.' Ruth glanced at her husband, as if daring him to stop her. 'Reuben asked me to marry him in one of those hay meadows. We'd only known each other three weeks. My parents were horrified when I told them, but I didn't care. I was tired of trailing around the world behind them. I was going to stay at Tithebarn with the man of my dreams . . .'

Reuben went on glowering at his glass. Sitting there like an unexploded bomb.

Katharine said, 'Bread and butter pudding, anyone? We're into all the old-fashioned puddings at the moment, aren't we, Ruthie? Cheap and cheerful, but our customers seem to like them. Simon, change the tape. Janacek, I think.'

It was Margaret Fleming who took the conversation on to the Bath Festival. 'Are you still on the Fringe committee? Only attendances were down, they tell me, and I'm sure that must be connected with some of the more peculiar things that were booked. Absolute flops, you must admit?'

'But you can't just stick to the conventional. The arts are about experiment.'

'The arts are about what people will pay to see. And that means more Mozart and less modern rubbish.'

Into Elizabeth's mind, with these words, sprang something that the box-office girl had told her, only yesterday, about the programme at the Theatre Royal. The shadow of a smile flitted across her face as she relished the thought of passing the information on to a certain lady not a hundred miles away, at some future date.

Katharine moved to the sideboard and, picking up the huge cheese dish, made room for it in the centre of the table. Then she fetched the port.

'The youngsters wouldn't agree with you, would they, Ruthie? Your Sal simply loves modern rubbish.'

It was Reuben who answered. 'Never stopped playing the blasted stuff. Like a cat being strangled . . . I don't know why she couldn't play rock and roll like anybody else.'

'Rock and roll?' Ruth said. 'That went out with the ark.'

'I wouldn't pretend to keep in touch with it like you do.'

Ruth was getting worked up. She stared at him dangerously. 'I don't pretend. I actually like to share Sal's interests. And the reason she prefers avant-garde music is that she's an intelligent, well-educated girl.'

'I should damned well hope so. Keeping her at that posh school cost a fortune.'

'Well, at least she got to university. Philly Lucas finished up mucking out horses.'

'You can't keep off the subject, can you?' Reuben's voice had suddenly grown rough.

'Cheese, anyone?' Katharine Ellerton cut in. 'Simon, pass round the biscuits. Mrs Blair, I understand you're setting up a quilting exhibition . . .?'

Ruth drained the contests of her glass. A beatific, if crafty, smile was crossing her face. She was drunk. Not so drunk that she didn't know what she was saying, but enough for all her inhibitions to have dropped away. 'What subject is that, dear? Your precious ex-girlfriend?'

There was a moment's nerve-racking silence, before Reuben said, 'Leave Jane out of this, you bitch!'

Ruth leaned forward, resting her chin on her hands. 'He's got a filthy temper when riled. Do you know, when he was at school, he knocked out a boy who was laughing at his rotten spelling?'

Oliver took advantage of the moment to pour himself another port. He was feeling no pain.

'He was as mad as hell when he found he'd got me pregnant. That was the reason he was forced to propose. You had to, in those days . . .'

Even Margaret's jaw dropped open at that one.

'Shall I tell you something else? Shall I tell you what they sprayed over the wall when they set the vehicles alight? REUBEN DANDO FUCKING BASTARD! Pretty funny really. Because they were immensely accurate.'

For a few seconds, Ruth seemed to be struggling with hysteria. Then she pushed her chair back. 'You'll have to excuse me. I think I'm going to be sick . . .'

19

Elizabeth creaked her way up the staircase and shivered a little.

'I'll see if she's OK,' she had told the others, a moment or two after Ruth's precipitate departure. She'd glanced in Reuben's direction on her way out of the dining-room. He had seemed transfixed, his face obdurately blank.

The first-floor landing smelled of musty hymn books. She imagined the Rectory as it was when a boarding school had been housed there during the war. With the huge, rattling windows scotch-taped and freezing cold dormitories. Some echo of that utilitarian time hung around the place.

The passage seemed to stretch for miles. There was a shadowy line of doors, several of them half open. Elizabeth had no idea where the bathroom was, so she began on the left and worked her way down. Ticked off the main bedroom (cluttered and untidy), James's (wall chart of Kings and Queens) and Letty's (flower-decorated with pony books), plus two other empty rooms before she found the one she wanted.

Ruth Dando hadn't bothered – or hadn't had time – to bolt the door. She was sitting on the floor in a bedraggled heap.

'Can I do anything?' Elizabeth asked.

'No. I'm all right.'

She didn't look all right. She looked like someone who had just heaved the contents of her stomach down the loo and flushed them away.

'Let me get you a coffee.'

'No. Really.' Ruth's voice slurred a little. 'I couldn't face it.'

'Some water, then.' Elizabeth found a tooth mug and filled it. 'Here. Just have a sip.'

Ruth did as she was told. 'You didn't tell me you worked for Max Shepard.'

'With, not for. There's a big difference.'

'You're right. I feel as if I've been working for Reuben all my life.' Then, lifting her head and blurting the words out, she said, 'I spoiled Kat's party. Well, I don't really care! I'm sick of worrying about what people will think.'

'You can do too much of it,' Elizabeth agreed.

'Let him put on his black face! I've seen it before.' She took another sip of the water. 'Shouldn't have said that about Philly. But it's some kind of comfort to know that his perfect woman made a right mess of bringing her daughter up.'

Elizabeth smiled awkwardly.

'Not that our Sal was always a little angel, but she had her head screwed on right . . . which is more than you could say for some.' She went gabbling on. 'I thought when he saw what a mess she'd made of bringing up Philly, it might enlighten him. Make him think less of her. But it had the opposite effect . . . made him feel protective, sorry for her. God, men are stupid!'

'It can seem like that.'

'All he ever wanted was to marry Jane, you see, but she went off and married someone else. I couldn't have turned up at a worse time. He'd have taken any girl who came along and offered herself. And then you spend a lifetime hating each other.'

'It can't all have been bad?'

Her face was paler than ever. 'Oh . . . not all of it, I suppose. It's just hard never being the centrepin of anyone's life. Not my parents'. They had each other, they didn't need me . . . Not Reuben's. Not Sal's, now that she's grown up and gone off. What's it all about, Mrs Blair? What's any of it about when you look at it hard?'

What did you say to that? Elizabeth seemed to be contemplating.

'Do you know what the worst thing is? Apart from this last few weeks, we've learned, over the years, to hide our emotions. Bury them under piles of chicken dung.' Her fingers began picking at the rug on the floor. 'The last time I tried to tell him I loved him – years ago now – he made me feel so stupid. After that, I grew a hard shell.

'And now . . .' She let out a long, shuddering breath. '. . . I hate him. One day, I even decided I'd join the ALF. I had so much anger inside me. I decided I'd like to help them put gelignite under his car. Blow him to kingdom come.' A hollow laugh. 'Just think what a field day the papers would have had . . .'

Elizabeth looked down at her. There was an odd expression on her face. Perhaps suspicion. Perhaps even pity. 'And did you?' she said.

'Set his van on fire? Of course not!'

'What about Joanna Drew's murder?'

'Did I aim for Jane and shoot Joanna?' A slight flicker of something lit up her eyes. 'Is it likely?' she asked.

'I don't know. I was asking you.'

'If I'd wanted to kill Jane – and believe me, I've felt like it – I'd have chosen an easier time and place. Like when she met him in the barn . . .'

'When was this?'

For a moment, Ruth's eyes looked away. Then she shrugged, as if she didn't care that she had let it out. 'A couple of months back. I felt sure he was meeting her regularly. He's not entirely devoid of poetry, you know. It's just that he keeps it all for his precious Jane. The barn was one of their old haunts when they were teenagers. He told me that years back. I could just imagine them in the hay together. And after a while, that kind of thought eats into you . . .'

'Why were they meeting in the barn?'

'Why do you think? I'm pretty sure they weren't discussing the egg yield!'

A short silence followed. Elizabeth found herself rearranging a lot of things inside her head.

'Was it just the once or more often than that?'

'It's been going on for years, for all I know.'

'But how many times did you actually see them? You did see them?'

'I'd suspected it for ages. Then one afternoon in September, I came across her car half hidden on the old mud track at the back of the barn. I knew she was in there with Reuben. I waited until they came out.'

'Did you confront them?'

'I didn't choose to.' There was no emotion, no feeling now, in the terse monotone.

'And were there other occasions?'

'Two, that I know of.'

'How long were they in there together?'

'An hour or so. I didn't time them. Long enough.'

Elizabeth didn't ask for what. It was obvious what Ruth meant. She gave Ruth a grave look. 'It was you who scratched Jane's car . . .'

Ruth looked distinctly defiant. 'Guilty! I took a knife to it and they thought it was the ALF. I got enormous pleasure out of doing that. I felt exhilarated for hours . . . I got rid of a lot of pent-up anger. It was as if I'd somehow rescued myself from the mess and grief of my marriage.'

'And was that all you did to rescue yourself?'

'That's all, I swear it.' Ruth was trying, as quickly as she could, to adjust her image from that of a criminal to a victim. 'I didn't kill Joanna. But Jane Maddocks isn't half so sweet and open as you think she is!'

'Which of us are?'

Ruth's voice developed a note of bitterness, a cold edge. 'I wish she had died that night. Because I don't know who I am any more, or what I'm doing here. God, I've got a headache. And I'm going to be sick again . . .'

When Elizabeth walked back down the stairs, Margaret Fleming was phoning for a taxi. 'How is she?'

'Being ill again.'

'Honestly, what an evening!'

'I've had more peaceful ones,' Elizabeth said. But not more interesting.

A silence fell as she entered the dining-room. 'I think you should take her home,' she started to say. But Reuben's chair was empty. 'Where is he?'

'Slammed off home,' Katharine told her. 'Said if she was going to behave like that, she could get a bloody taxi. Sorry, Simon . . .'

'Quite right, too,' said Oliver, firmly but drunkenly. 'She made him look foolish.'

Margaret said, 'Oliver – your coat's in the hall. Lovely meal, Katharine. You must come to us next time.'

'Well, that was a different kind of evening,' Elizabeth said ruefully as the cab drove out of the Rectory gates. 'I'm sorry, dear. It's normally a pretty civilized place.'

'Marriage', Hal said, 'is rarely civilized.'

'Perhaps you're right.' Startlingly, heavily, in the pitch black, the church clock struck twelve.

Hal thought for a moment. 'Well, you know what they say.'

'What do they say, Hal?'

'If you can't have a good marriage, have a good divorce.'

Elizabeth smiled, but in truth, she scarcely heard what he had said. She peered out at the dark hedgerows, making imaginary jottings on a notebook inside her head.

Reuben Dando. Motive for killing Joanna Drew – blackmail? She'd found out about the affair with Jane and was threatening to tell Tom. Weak, even taking into account Joanna's instability. What could Tom have done, if she had told him? Anyway, Reuben would have been proud for the relationship to come out into the open. (Re. blackmail, check on his finances.)

Alternative theory: Reuben found out about Jane's affair with Nick, was jealous, went to shoot Jane and Joanna got in the way. Motive stronger, but his subsequent behaviour doesn't fit, though. Unless he's shamming the concern for Jane.

Jane . . . always Jane. Can't see her involved in Joanna's murder, but she's sure as hell always there in the centre of things.

Strange how, tonight, Reuben and Ruth's roles reversed themselves. She taking the upper hand, he retreating in the face of it. Interesting, that. It makes you wonder what would happen if . . .

Hal began to snore quietly in the seat beside her. She didn't wake him. He'd be up in the small hours with jet lag, poor old thing.

The taxi ambled on up the hill. She went back to her note-making.

Ruth Dando. Motive for wanting to kill Jane as plain as the nose on your face. Deep, long-term hatred of Jane. Revenge on her husband. Odd thought: what would she do if she found out that Joanna had been blackmailing Reuben? Memo: Get Max's policeman friend to check on Tithebarn account sheets. Ruth wouldn't care if Reuben was paying for his extra-marital affair, but she might if lack of finances threatened her own lifestyle. Or her business.

Tom Maddocks. Might have been driven to kill his wife if he found out she's been having a string of affairs. Blind jealousy. Trouble is, it's hard to see the urbane Tom in the guise of jealous lover.

Can you see him murdering his own sister for the insurance money? Not really . . .

The taxi was turning now into the lane that led to Elizabeth's cottage. Hal muttered something incoherently in his sleep. Jerked himself awake and blinked hard.

'It's all right, dear. We're home.'

'Home? I'm not home. Where the devil am I?'

'We're passing Dottie's greenhouse. What you need . . . what we both need . . . is a cup of good, strong coffee.'

'Amen to that,' said Hal, as the taxi came to a sudden stop.

The duvet was very large and very warm and very, very cosy. It excluded every bit of cold that there could be in the universe. And then some.

'Suppose we stay here for ever?' said Max. (He'd been amazed and profoundly honoured when she crept into his room a couple of hours earlier.)

'You'd get bored.' Helen lay with her body half turned towards him. Her hair smelled of honey and oranges.

'Want to bet?'

Her mouth tilted into a tiny smile. 'Would I lose it?'

'You most certainly would.'

'Then I won't bet. I'll believe you.'

'Good.'

'Max . . .'

'Helen . . .'

'Can I ask you something?'

'Ask away.'

Indecision hovered over her face. Max felt like taking it between his hands and kissing all those grave doubts away. But he held himself back. What she desperately needed was verbal reassurance. The other kind didn't last long enough to help.

'I want to know what you think he'll do next.'

'Liam?'

'Yes. I can't stand not knowing.'

'Listen, we've talked about this. The children are protected by the courts now. And I've got a thick file on him, remember? The lawyers would make mincemeat of him.'

'The courts didn't stop him before.'

'Well, they will now. Anyway, I'm here to protect you.'

'Yes.' Helen's mouth twitched in what was almost a smile.

Max drew her in closer to him. He had a sudden inspiration. 'Listen – we'll go off somewhere for a break . . . all four of us. Somewhere romantic, somewhere the kids will have fun.'

'Somewhere in the sun?' Her head was on his shoulder now, her voice sounded almost sleepy.

'Would you like that?'

'Mmmm.'

'Then we'll get some brochures tomorrow.' To hell with the fact that he couldn't afford it. If it would relax her, make her eyes brighten . . . His voice was husky. 'Helen . . .'

The urge to make love to her again was uncontrollable.

Helen turned in his arms and melted against him.

Her bare skin against his. 'God, Helen –'

The phone shrilled. *Bloody hell!*

'Yes! What is it?'

Silence. But a threatening kind of silence. Someone was out there.
'Who was it?' asked Helen, when he put down the receiver.
'Wrong number,' Max told her.
She didn't believe him.

20

At ten the next morning, Milson Street was already buzzing with Christmas shoppers. The sky was gloomy, but the windows were all glittering. Elizabeth was walking down to Martha Washington, when she spotted a familiar figure across the street. Just the person I wanted to see, she thought. But Margaret Fleming seemed bent on looking the other way.

'Hey, Mrs Fleming!' Elizabeth called across to her. 'Good morning.'

Margaret was a moment deciding that she had now to acknowledge Elizabeth's presence. Before that, she turned and said something to Oliver, who was standing by their car.

'You're early birds!' Elizabeth said cheerfully. 'So what brings you out at this hour? Caught many worms?'

As she crossed the road, she saw that Oliver's expression was frayed. He stood clasping the car keys tight into his palm.

Margaret smiled frigidly. 'We've been to the bank.'

'Both of you? Don't tell me, you've been checking how much your husband's been spending!'

'Not at all.' Margaret actually took her at her word. There was no mistaking it: she looked thoroughly uneasy.

Oliver smiled nervously in Elizabeth's direction and glanced at his watch.

'I was only joking, you know.'

'It's a little early for jokes.'

'I'm so sorry. You're quite right. But I've got this problem with my brain. Comes of getting old, you know. The grey cells are dying.'

Out of the corner of his eye, Oilver shot a glance at Margaret, whose face had become as blank as a wall. He was like a cat on hot bricks. Couldn't wait to cut and run.

140

'Oh . . . by the way . . . I meant to ask . . .' Elizabeth turned on the charm and smiled at Margaret. Smiled with a look of pure innocence in her green eyes. 'I bumped into an old friend the other night. A theatre-going friend. And it's an odd thing, but she went to see *The Recruiting Officer* on the night of Joanna Drew's murder. You were telling me how much you enjoyed it . . .'

'Yes.'

'You mentioned the eighteenth-century costumes, I believe?'

'Yes, they were quite stunning.' Oliver, barely three paces away, seemed to stiffen. Margaret's voice betrayed nothing but a hint of wariness.

'It was a dual bill, wasn't it, that week? Two plays, alternating.'

'So I believe.' Still Margaret's face showed no response.

'Well, it's an odd thing – I don't quite understand it, but my friend said they had some kind of technical hitch on the night she went. They couldn't do *The Recruiting Officer* so they had to swap plays and do the alternative one instead. In modern dress . . .'

No answer. Oliver was wetting himself.

'One of you must have got the date wrong. But it couldn't have been my friend, because she showed me her ticket.'

Elizabeth shook her head as if puzzled. She went to turn away and then stopped. 'By the way, did I tell you that the police are trying to trace a woman who called at Joanna Drew's cottage at around eight on the night she was murdered? No? I must have forgotten. Well, I must be getting on. Customers to see to . . .'

She strolled off down the street, leaving the pavement now and again to avoid the crowds. She turned just the once, as she reached the junction with Quiet Street. Margaret was in the driving seat with the engine running. There was something coming, so she couldn't pull out yet.

The car stopped, let her move out. She gave a half-wave, let the clutch out hard, stalled it, slammed the brake on.

Oliver seemed to be praying as he stared at the traffic that was jammed up behind them. At last, Margaret shot off down the street. A car honked as she accelerated past the spot where Elizabeth stood.

Yes, Margaret had seen her, as she turned her head to look down Quiet Street. I've worked it out, Elizabeth thought. The reason why you praised Joanna Drew to the skies when we first met. You didn't want anyone to know how you really felt about her.

141

And now you're sweating. Well, I can wait. You can stew for a while. And then we'll see . . .

Helen was already up when the alarm went off. She was wandering around the kitchen in silk pyjamas that were miles too big for her.

'Coffee?' She smiled at him. *She looks like she belongs here,* thought Max, and that made him happy.

'Mmm.' He went over to put his arms around her.

'You won't get it like this.'

'I won't bother then,' Max said. 'You OK? I mean you're not worrying?'

'No,' Helen said. She looked away from him, out of the window. 'Like you said, he'd only land up in jail.'

'Good girl. Anyway, he doesn't know where you are.'

She said nothing.

He glanced at the clock on the wall. 'Eight fifteen. I've got to go.'

'Not until you've had breakfast.'

'No time. I'll just have coffee.'

The sun was shining, filling the whole place with shimmering warmth. As he took a shower and threw his clothes on, he felt light-headed with happiness. Not at all shagged out as usual in the mornings. The kids were making one hell of a din in the hall, but he didn't give a damn. It was a funny thing how your whole life could change in the blink of an eyelid.

'I think I'm getting a cold,' she said as he kissed her goodbye.

'Go back to bed.'

'I can't. I ought to get the kids back to school.'

'Leave it until next week,' he said. 'Let them settle.'

'Perhaps you're right.' She held on to him for a moment. He could feel her warmth through the silk.

The legs hurrying along the pavement above the area steps were getting faster and more frequent. 'I'll have to go,' he said again.

'I know.'

'I'll ring you later. And stop worrying! OK?'

'OK.'

It made him feel odd, leaving a family at home. The thought

142

buzzed and fizzed inside him as he strode along Great Pulteney Street. Leaving the children and Helen. The morning was filled with winter sunlight and with her perfume . . .

Later that same day, Ruth Dando stood alone in the yard, under a lowering sky. The air was keen. The wind smelled alternatively of the woods and of sour chicken droppings.

Ruth was remembering Tithebarn as it used to be, remembering what it felt like to wander down across the cobbles, climb the stile and take the footpath down to the old barn. She saw again the pear tree that used to stand in one corner of the walled garden (now covered by offices). Saw, in her mind's eye, the pinkish gleam of blossom against honeyed stone.

Tithebarn when it was Tithebarn . . .

Tithebarn when there was a sea of cow parsley down below the orchard. And skylarks, instead of the dull, perpetual hum of generators.

Above the farm, the hill leaned at an alarming angle. It seemed to look down on the battery sheds with a stern eye. A fringe of bare beeches raised itself into the sky like an arched brow.

There was this film running inside her head. A film that had the gremlins in it. It kept stopping and starting, so that she had been feeling, for hours, excited, yet frightened at the same time. Dizzy. Almost ill. In short, disconnected flashes, she could see what she was about to do . . .

She closed her eyes, giving in to the desire to drift somewhere far away from it all. But there were voices, down there below in the Gatehouse, which kept interrupting. Voices saying, '. . . ADS. We're losing too many. Got to get the percentage down . . .'

ADS. Acute death syndrome . . . connected with too-rapid growth. The birds lose their balance, get strong muscular contractions. Shortly before death, they do flip-overs on to their backs.

Acute death syndrome . . . Ruth would have laughed at the irony of it, if it wasn't all so surreal.

Someone was saying, '. . . not a legal requirement at the moment . . .' Then the voice faded away and another – more local – one said, '. . . number 3 was a madhouse yesterday . . .'

Ruth opened her eyes with some effort and the battery sheds

143

were still squatting there. The floodlights quivered and swayed and finally put themselves back on top of the grim, wire-topped walls.

She fingered the scrap of paper in her pocket. Tried to control the convulsions inside her stomach.

After a long time, she walked towards the car . . .

Elizabeth glanced out of the shop window. It was almost dark out in the mews, but the sky still showed a livid grey up high against the roof-tops and it wasn't yet quite dark. Not long before closing time.

The Turkey Tracks quilt was still in the window, its myriad prints in red and rich reds and greens a feast to the eye. And a lesson in balancing colour tones. She stared at it broodingly. The transition from light to dark at the square ends was so subtle that from a distance the dark pieces appeared to be moulded.

If you squinted hard or gazed at it long enough, a third overall design emerged. And it was exactly the same with the Wetherburn murders. Emerging and receding forms floating around in your mind and just when you thought you'd got hold of one, you had to blink and it disappeared again.

She sighed and called out to Caroline. 'I'd better start cashing up. Can't find my reading specs. You see them?'

'They were on the table earlier.'

They were on the table now, half hidden by the teacups. 'Found them,' she said. Then, 'I'm chilled. Are you?'

'My nose is.' Caroline appeared from the back room, shrugging on her coat. 'Like an icebox. Where's your brother today?' she asked in that polite, ladylike voice of hers.

'He's gone off pumpkin hunting.'

'Oh, really?' Caroline opened her eyes even wider than usual.

'To make a Thanksgiving pie. Nothing to do with glass slippers.'

'Oh, I see,' Caroline said hastily, turning rather pink.

'Though he's been gone so long, I suspect he may have called in at a local hostelry.'

'Oh, right,' said Caroline, buttoning herself in. 'I'll be off then, Mrs B. See you in the morning.'

But as she got half-way to the door, the phone rang, so she stopped and picked it up.

'It's a Mr Fleming,' she said to Elizabeth, when the other person had stopped speaking.

'*Oliver* Fleming?'

'Yes. He wants to see you. Tonight, preferably. Can you come to his house? Would seven-ish suit?'

Elizabeth felt a fierce, sudden spark inside her. 'Tell him yes. We'll both be there. Write down the address. And don't go for two minutes. I want to pop upstairs.'

She ran, quickly, up the stairs to Max's office. He was standing by the window with his hands in his pockets. He turned, slowly, as she burst in.

'Couldn't we go another day?' he asked, when she told him about the call.

'And risk Oliver changing his mind? No way!'

'Couldn't you go on your own? I want to get home early.'

'Listen, Max –' She must have looked fierce, because he held up a hand.

'All right, all right. But no longer than half an hour . . . OK?'

Hal was in a mellow state when he marched back in with the pumpkin. He couldn't tell her where he'd been or how he'd found his way back. He figured it was best, in new places, to wander.

'You'd better have some tea,' Elizabeth said. 'And put that thing down before you drop it.'

21

Oliver Fleming's gold signet ring lifted as he nervously fingered his chin. He shifted uncomfortably in his chair. Max said, 'You wanted to see us.'

'Yes. Yes, I did.' He found a smile, but there wasn't much power to it and it flickered out again.

'Is it about the murders?'

'In a manner of speaking.'

The clock struck silver chimes. With an enquiring look on his face, Max sat there waiting. He remembered one of Elizabeth's favourite expressions. Fleming was as jumpy as a jack rabbit.

'You obviously know that my wife lied about her whereabouts on the night Joanna was murdered.'

'Yes. Elizabeth told me.'

'Well, I've decided that if the truth has to come out . . . well, I'd rather talk to you than to the police. Perhaps it's our only chance. Damage limitation, don't you see?'

Elizabeth made only the slightest movement in her chair, then sat there waiting for Fleming to go on.

'It's hard to know where to start.' Oliver's eye was evasive, his hands trembled.

'Let's start with Joanna Drew. Were you friends?'

'Joanna didn't have friends. Only acquaintances. She was a cold woman.'

'Nevertheless . . . I've been told you had regular . . . and secret . . . assignations with Joanna Drew.'

Oliver's eyes shot up. 'Who told you that?'

'It doesn't matter. Is it true?'

A long silence. Then, 'Yes. Yes . . .' The words were faint, almost a whisper.

'Were you having an affair with Mrs Drew?'

'Good God, no!' Oliver looked shocked.

'Did your wife know about the assignations?'

Another silence. 'Yes. Yes, she did.'

'Let me ask you another question. Was Joanna blackmailing you?'

'Why do you say that?' Oliver's face had gone paper white.

'Call it information received. Let's change tack, then. You were very friendly with Jane Maddocks. I understand you used to visit her in the evenings. Was that relationship closer than it should have been?'

'Look – what is this?' Unable to contain his indignation, Oliver brought his hand down on the desk. 'A sleazy tabloid investigation? I wasn't having an affair with anyone. Good God, I wouldn't have the energy, for one thing.'

'Nevertheless, Joanna was blackmailing you. And your wife visited her cottage on the night she was murdered. Tim Quennell saw her. It was your wife, wasn't it?'

This time, the silence was as heavy as lead.

'I . . . He must have been mistaken. It was dark.'

Elizabeth said, '*He* may not be sure. I am. Otherwise, why would she tell the police she went to the theatre when she didn't?'

A pause. 'Look – I . . . I don't want my wife brought into this . . . Not at all. Do you hear?'

'I need to talk to her about this crime . . . these crimes, Mr Fleming.'

'No – you can't. It's me you need to talk to. I'll tell you all I know. But Margaret wasn't involved in those murders.'

His voice was desperate and his eyes, as he stared back at them across the desk, seemed to be those of a frightened child. Max leaned back in his chair; his face was impassive. He took his time fishing the tape recorder from his pocket.

'All right. All right. I'll tell you why Joanna was blackmailing me. Oh, God . . . I don't know where to start.'

Another voice spoke from the doorway behind them. 'Start with your mother.'

It was Margaret Fleming, dressed in an elderly tweed jacket and looking older, less official. She seemed to have lost weight and she had definitely missed her weekly appointment with the hair-dresser.

'Better if you tell him everything,' she said wearily. 'You've had one heart attack. The stress of all this could bring on another.'

A chill seemed to have settled over the room. Oliver nervously fiddled with his cufflinks. Even the tree outside the window was restless in the wind.

'If you say so, Margaret. My mother . . .' He gave a dry cough and started again. 'My mother and I were close. Very close . . . My father died in a drowning accident, you see, when I was only six years old and she had a terrific struggle bringing me up. Financially, I mean. She was determined I should go to the same public school as my father did – minor public school – so she scrimped and saved to pay the fees. Borrowed some money from an unmentionable uncle and damned near starved to keep me there . . . She was a wonderful woman. Beautiful and she had such spirit and taught me so many things. She lived for me, I suppose, after Father died.'

Margaret was leaning against the window, gripping the radiator hard.

'Well, there was this intensely close attachment between my mother and me. Margaret resented it sometimes, I know that. But it was there and somehow she managed to put up with it.'

'Get on with it, Oliver. No detours.'

'No detours . . .' His gaze went to the greenish panes of the window. 'We'll get to the point, then. My mother developed senile dementia when she was only seventy. I was devastated. She didn't shuffle along like an old woman. The disease hadn't reached that stage. But she began to forget things . . . and invent things that never happened. It's such a cruel disease. Sometimes she would look at me and say, "Who are you?" I was only glad she couldn't see herself in such a sad state. She would have hated it. She had always been such a proud, graceful woman. Margaret wanted me to put her in a home, but I wasn't having that. She'd looked after me and I was damned well going to look after her . . . until the end, no matter how difficult it got.'

'And it got bloody difficult.' It was with a flat, hard voice that Margaret cut in.

'You had to watch her every minute of the day or she just went off. Wandered all over the place.' Oliver looked at Elizabeth, then away again. 'It was a weight and an anguish, but somehow you had to cope with it. I felt protective towards her, as if she were now the child . . .'

He was paler than ever. The room at the back of the old house was deadly quiet as he went on with his story. 'One day . . . well, I'd taken her out for a drive and I stopped at the local supermarket to pick up one or two things. I left Mother in the car . . . locked in, I thought. But while I was in the shop, I caught a glimpse of her out of the corner of my eye, wandering out of the car park. I dashed out to stop her, without thinking. And somehow I'd got a couple of packs of batteries in my pocket. Well, the long and the short of it was, they didn't believe my story about Mother. I was arrested for shoplifting.

'It went to the Crown Court. I refused to plead guilty. And I felt sure that a jury would believe my story, but they didn't. They thought I was using my mother's illness as an excuse. Plenty do, I suppose. Anyway, I was fined and received a suspended prison sentence.' Oliver's nerves were obviously stretched about as far as they would go. He looked at Margaret as if to say, 'Help me.' But she had turned to stare out of the window, as if she couldn't bear to face them any longer.

'I had to resign my job because of it. And then, six months later, Mother died – she had a fall and broke her hip – and I applied for the job here at the Wetherburn. I thought, if we moved far enough away . . .' His voice petered off. 'Anyway, to cut a long story short, when I filled in the application form, I didn't mention the shoplifting conviction. Well, you don't have to, you know, unless you're applying for certain kinds of jobs . . . like working with children or dealing primarily with money. I knew I wouldn't stand a chance if I owned up.

'It was very wrong of me not to own up on the form, but it was a moment's impulse . . . I stuck it in the postbox before I could change my mind. I have to look after Margaret, you see. I have to earn a living.' Leaden-faced, Oliver gazed across at Max. 'The rest you know. I got the job, left my past behind me in Cambridge. But all these years we've been holding our breath in case someone walked into the Wetherburn who recognized me from our old life.'

'That was seven years ago.' Margaret Fleming was facing them now. 'And everything went along fine until Joanna found out about Oliver's conviction. God knows how, but she was that kind of woman. Liked to pry out your failings – and then use them against you. She was blackmailing Oliver and forcing him to connive at doctoring the Wetherburn books.'

'Doctoring the books?' Max was startled out of his silence.

'She'd been borrowing money from Wetherburn funds to cover her gambling debts, I believe. She didn't want Tom to find out. Anyway, all I had to do was keep my mouth shut and keep moving the money around. Sleight of hand, so that Tom never found out about it.'

And what if Tom had found out? Elizabeth wondered. Would he have been angry enough to take his revenge on his sister? She gazed across at Margaret Fleming. 'So when you visited Joanna at her cottage that night . . .?'

'I went to beg her to leave Oliver alone. But I didn't kill her, I swear it.' Margaret's cool façade had cracked at last. 'I was going to tell her he couldn't take much more. It was taking a toll on his health. He was eating badly, sleeping badly. I was terrified he was going to have another heart attack.'

'But you're saying that you didn't see her?'

'She wasn't there, I tell you! The lights were on and the back door was unlocked, but I couldn't make anyone hear. I looked upstairs, but it seemed empty, so I waited for a while, thinking that she'd gone out with the dogs. When she didn't come back, I gave up and went home.' She was trying to speak calmly, but her voice was full

149

of panic. Her fingers kept twisting at the tissue she was holding, screwing it round and round until it was a tight little ball. 'I was scared to tell the police I was there in case they started to delve into Oliver's background. If they'd interviewed him . . . well, you know what he's like. Lord knows what he'd have dropped out. I had to keep protecting him, you see. You've got to believe me. I didn't kill Joanna.'

'Can you think of anyone else who might have? Someone else she might have been blackmailing, for instance?'

'Not on the spur of the moment.' An odd look crossed her face. 'Well, actually, there was something . . . Something that puzzled me. I was down in the basement one day, when I heard Joanna arguing with that Anderson fellow.'

'Ted Anderson?'

'Yes. They seemed to be having quite a barney. I couldn't catch much of it . . . but Nick Quennell's name was mentioned.'

Oliver said, 'What we've just told you . . . Will it have to go further? I mean . . . the police?'

'I don't see any reason to tell them. As long as they don't come asking . . .'

A slow flush crept up over his face. He might survive, after all. It was as if his whole body was coming back to life. 'Thank you.' His voice was shaking. 'Thank you.'

'No problem.'

Elizabeth walked back down the staircase behind Margaret with a thoughtful look on her face. When they reached the hall, she stopped and held out her hand.

'Thanks for your time,' she said.

Margaret merely hunched her shoulders. 'Oliver didn't give me much choice. I just hope you can keep your promise to him, that's all.' She hesitated, then suddenly blurted out, 'That woman was a poisoned spider, spinning and weaving her evil web.'

'Yes, well . . .'

'I'm glad she's dead and that's the truth.'

'You wouldn't be the only one.'

'He didn't deserve what she did to him. He just didn't deserve it!'

Her lower lip trembled and her eyes filled. Harsh tears ran down her cheeks. It was so unexpected, so almost touching, that Elizabeth gripped her shoulder.

'Try not to worry,' was all she could say.

At the same moment, the front door opened and Jane Maddocks blew in with a huge armful of files. She was apparently surprised to see them. 'There's nothing wrong, is there? Margaret – what on earth's the matter?'

'Nothing's the matter,' Margaret said. 'Nothing at all. I wish Tom would get that door fixed. Banging away every time someone walks in. All it needs is a rubber stop behind it. Wouldn't take five minutes . . .'

Jane's eyes were baffled as she watched Margaret charge off back upstairs. 'There *is* something wrong. I never expected to see Margaret in tears. Not in a million years . . .'

'We all have our breaking points,' Elizabeth said.

'I know. But Margaret – I thought she was . . . well, impregnable.'

Her grey eyes were uncomprehending, almost apprehensive as they gazed up the stairs. 'I suppose,' she said, 'it gets to us all in the end?'

Elizabeth had to agree. Suddenly she couldn't wait to get out of the place. She felt she had had enough of it.

There were moments when she wished she had never been drawn up there. All those shiny floors, slippery with wax. All those slippery emotions . . .

22

Elizabeth hitched her boots out of the cupboard. There had been a sprinkling of snow overnight and more was on the way. A buffeting north wind was roaring around the woods and gardens.

'Going out?' Hal's rangy form came out of the sitting-room as she banged the cupboard door.

'I thought we'd take a nice, blowy walk. Up through the woods.'

He gave her a suspicious look. 'A walk?' he said. 'How far?'

She decided to string him along. 'Just a little trot. Ten miles or so.'

'Forget it! I'm still jet-lagged.'

'You're still bone idle. Come on! It's not far. I was kidding you. There'll be an interesting surprise at the end.'

He grumbled some more, but in the end, he gave in.

It was too cold to saunter. They took the rough track that led up behind the Manor to the old railway embankment at a good, licking pace until they were deep inside Greystone Wood. Here, the sound of the wind was louder. It was like being on a galleon sailing in a force ten gale, she thought, with all that creaking timber. To the right lay wave after wave of blowing woods; to the left, windswept fields.

'Reminds me of that tornado Jim and I got caught up in,' Elizabeth said.

'Tornado?'

'Late one afternoon. We were out in the car. I wanted him to put his foot down, but he wouldn't. Never, ever, try to outrun it by driving, he said, because it will always go much faster than you can get up to. So we sat it out. I was scared half to death.'

The path ahead was slippery. Covered in a fine dusting of white. Elizabeth picked her way along it with care. At the top, in a small clearing, she bent forward to examine something else that vividly reminded her of Virginia. Tracks in the snow, leading across to the copse at the edge of the wood.

'Wild turkey,' Hal said. 'Should have brought my gun.'

'No, not wild turkey. You don't get those here. It must have escaped from one of the farms.' Church Farm, probably. Not Tithebarn. Nothing ever escaped from Tithebarn.

Turkey tracks . . . Windows in Elizabeth's memory opened one after the other. 'Remember Grandfather raising turkeys for the Thanksgiving slaughter?' she said.

'I remember the one that chased you into the house.'

'One of those disagreeable old yard birds. I was seven years old. And I was glad when it got butchered.' The birds had hung on a beam in the big, red barn and were plucked in the kitchen a day later.

She remembered something else. 'Amos and Mary Pulaski always came in to help. And the turkey feathers flew all over the place.'

Amos and Mary Pulaski . . . They had quilted as a team for all the craft fairs.

'Amos is turning arthritic,' Hal told her.

'Poor old thing. Last time I was home, he told me, "I just do the quilting. Mary's the artist. She's the one that makes the light shine." '

Obscurely, that drew her mind back to the Wetherburn. 'I wonder who makes the light shine in the Maddocks household?' she said, talking to herself rather than Hal. 'If it *is* still shining, that is . . .'

Hal didn't know what she was talking about. She didn't bother to enlighten him, but went on musing out loud. 'I mean, her affair with Quennell might have dimmed it somewhat. If Tom knew about it, that is. I just can't decide whether their new togetherness is a sham or not.'

They emerged from the trees. Stood looking down on the Wetherburn, which was half hidden by bare beeches. Scaffolding still spoiled the fine lines of the back wing. The lake was faintly blue, almost grey. There were swans below the boathouse . . .

'At least we don't eat those beautiful creatures any more,' Elizabeth said.

'Huh?'

'Swans. I was reading this cookery book the other night. No medieval feast was complete without a hefty sixteen-pound swan. So landowners began to "acquire" wild swans. They identified them by cutting notches, initials or heraldic emblems on their bills with a sharp knife.'

'That's bad,' said Hal.

'Oh, the twentieth century didn't invent cruelty to animals, that's for sure.'

She followed him down the slope, catching, as she did so, a glimpse of Joanna Drew's cottage in the valley below the lake. From here, you could trace Joanna's movements on the night she was murdered. Out of the cottage gate and along the lane. Over the stile, and up across the humpbacked field to the latched gate in the Wetherburn hedge. From there, she would have gone up across the lawn and round the side of the house to the boathouse. Something up there had caught her attention. A torch, perhaps, or some movement.

Joanna, who was the bright one of the family . . . Brighter than her brother Tom, or so he would have you think.

They trekked on, down over the field and across a cart track that led to another small copse. There was something on the path in front of them. A rabbit carcass . . . its eyes taken out by magpies. Elizabeth looked at the gaping holes, the half-eaten flesh, and winced.

'Survival of the fittest,' Hal said.

'And God help the rest . . .'

Elizabeth averted her gaze. The survival game . . . Everyone played it once or twice in life. Anyone would kill, if pushed into a tight enough corner.

At the end of the copse was a wire fence and the road, but try as they might, they couldn't find a stile. In the end, Elizabeth pressed down the bottom wire, shoved a leg through and climbed out on to the grass verge.

Hal had more trouble, but eventually he managed to squeeze himself through. 'Where are we heading for?' he asked, brushing himself down.

'Ted Anderson's farmhouse. It's down there in the trees.'

Elizabeth set off down the hill. There wasn't much to be seen between here and Anderson's land. Whitening hedgerows, a signpost, a wintry sun dropping down over the horizon. And a red car emerging from Anderson's drive.

Jane Maddocks drew up alongside them and wound down the window. 'Braving the elements?' She was evidently surprised to see them. 'You're a long way from home.'

'I guess you think we're mad.'

'I didn't exactly say that. If you're quick, you'll catch one of Ted's PAN sessions. He'd be delighted to see you. He's a bit light on customers in this weather. I'd have stayed myself – it's very soothing – but I only came up to drop Philly off.'

'Philly?'

'Yes. She has these sudden impulses . . .' She glanced at her watch. 'Well, you'll have to excuse me. I promised Tom I'd be back by three.'

'Be real careful on the hill,' Elizabeth said. The road was whitening fast.

'Don't worry,' she said. 'I'll crawl all the way.'

'What's all this about PAN sessions?' Hal said darkly.

'Didn't I tell you? We're going to try some deep meditation.'

'Like hell we are!' Hal said.

But Elizabeth, stepping briskly so as to get her seized-up joints moving again, was already turning in through Anderson's gates.

The farm was no longer a farm, though the two houses, one joined on to the back of the other, still stood, foursquare, in the middle of a fair old acreage.

The front part was used for the business, the back for living quarters. Jane Maddocks had been right about the welcome they would receive. Anderson came dashing out to greet them, calling to someone inside, 'Beth – two more chairs. Wonderful to see you . . . Come in, come in . . .'

They were late, but it didn't matter. Never mind about the paperwork. Deal with that later. Today they were focusing on infinity. Shrink the world, step right off it, let the radiance bloom. There was something manic about his excited enthusiasm . . .

The room into which he led them was stiflingly warm; there was a huge log-burning stove over at the far end. Anderson's wife was passing round a bowl of wine and chanting some mumbo-jumbo as she did so. Her blonde hair streamed out over her green, hippyish tunic and a seraphic smile touched the corners of her mouth. A dozen people sat around the white-covered table with their heads bent. After he had shown them to their places, Ted began lighting candles over in the corner, holding the taper with long, fine-boned fingers.

Hal seemed to be finding it difficult not to laugh. And it really was more comic than mystical. The incense they were burning had the same smell as the shop in Walcot Street. From where she sat, Elizabeth could see a picture of a screaming fish propped up against the wall.

Candles flickered and bobbed. When the chanting was finished, Anderson put on a tape of Indian music and began to read from the book in front of him.

Wang, wang . . .

'. . . stars in the Milky Way, fly with us . . .'

Wang, wang . . .

'. . . through fields of crystal with no flaws . . .'

His mouth made a little O as he drew breath. Elizabeth felt a giggle rising. Turned her head away – and saw, suddenly, at the end of the table, a face that she recognized.

Tim Quennell? With Philly Lucas. Today she was all in black – all anarchist chic. What the hell were they doing here together? Not communing, that was for sure. His eye caught her own. Peace and light? Forget it! That was anger and turbulence glaring back at her.

Now it was water that was being passed around, like at some pagan communion service. More incantations, recitations, ritual . . . not much of it making any sense. Then, finally, a kind of homespun blessing.

The session was, at long last, coming to an end.

Anderson was telling everyone to sit in free-fall for a moment, when Tim Quennell came to life. He leapt to his feet. 'You bloody hypocrite!' he yelled.

'Excuse me?' Anderson was now playing a different role. Smooth-man extraordinary. Executive management.

'No, I bloody won't excuse you . . . Maybe you can fool everyone else, but you don't fool me!'

'Look – do you have some problem? Because in that case –'

'Yes, I do have a problem.'

'Then maybe if we could adjourn to a –'

'No, we won't adjourn. We'll deal with it here!'

'Deal with what?'

'This!' Tim whipped a glass bottle from his pocket and slammed it hard on to the table. 'Why did you tell him that this rubbish would help my mother? How come you try to charge a fortune for this . . . this coloured cat's piss?'

They all sat there, frozen, waiting for him to answer.

'I . . . don't know what you're talking about.' Anderson had gone pale. He was shooting desperate glances in his wife's direction.

'Oh, no? Well, we're talking about all those lies you told. All the half-baked crap you tell people to make them buy your so-called healing potions.'

'Listen – I –'

'Listen? You must be joking!' Tim was now shaking with fury. 'My mother's slowly dying. And the stuff you told him to give her made her as sick as hell. It's prolonging her agony. I could kill you, you charlatan!'

Tim shoved his chair back, swung at Anderson, but missed.

'Tim. No –' Philly was trying to haul him off, but Tim hit Anderson a hard blow across the face, so that he crashed backwards and finally went down.

'Tim – for God's sake –'

Anderson sat there on the stone-flagged floor. Then he tried to haul himself up. 'I'd like you to leave my house,' he said.

'I bet you bloody would! And I'd like the police to investigate your so-called healing sessions. There's one more thing I want to

156

know. Did you work it out between you to get rid of her more quickly? Because if so –'

'Tim, stop it!' the girl yelled. 'You're not making sense!'

'Since when did anything have to make sense? Tell me that?'

She forced him out of the room, while Elizabeth stood thoughtfully fingering her spectacle case. Anderson and his wife were all apologies. 'Sorry about that,' Mrs Anderson said. Her restless green eyes didn't match the seraphic smile. 'You know how it is. Sometimes we attract oddballs.'

'I'm sure you must.' Elizabeth's gaze caught at a pile of children's books in the window sill. She found a smile. 'So where's your daughter today? The one that Jane's so fond of.'

'Persephone? Oh, we have a girl who looks after her while we work. We couldn't let her run about in here while we hold meetings. She'd make far too much noise. Atmosphere's so essential for spiritual healing.'

'Yes, it must be.' Poor little thing, Elizabeth thought. Shut away, so that she doesn't get in the way.

It was then that she had one of those strange flashes of insight. It was then that she saw it. Dogs . . . Persephone . . . Peter Robbing Paul . . . Jane's exotic Indian scarf . . . It was like a cold breeze running over the soul.

A theory had formed inside her head, ripening, growing, pushing all her previous theories out into the cold. It was like somebody had switched a light on.

As they let themselves out of the farmhouse, Hal started shaking his head.

'You're sure getting an education . . .' Elizabeth told him. 'It's interesting, though, isn't it?'

'That's not quite the word I'd choose,' Hal said.

Now it was snowing and raining at the same time. They sat off briskly for home. Strange, she thought, how these things come to you. It's like looking for oil wells. You get to a lot of dry holes before you find a gusher.

She couldn't wait to talk to Max. But before that, she had some letters to write . . .

23

Reuben's respiration wouldn't return to normal. He felt as if he'd been struck by lightning and he wasn't earthed.

He set off across the field with his dog. If he walked hard enough, he would grow more calm, the pulse in his head would stop banging.

The dog was growling at a rabbit hole, scratching at it with his paws and whining – anything to get in there, once he'd got the scent.

'Come away!' roared Reuben. His quick-moving gaze (the only thing that was quick about him) inspected the horizon. Dark trunks of trees . . . No one up there, but he kept looking anyway. You couldn't be too careful . . . Couldn't let down your guard.

His hands felt strange and there was a discomfort in his chest. Anxiety, not heartburn. A sudden panic clutched at him . . . What did she know? What had she told them? His body went on automatic pilot while his mind shot into all sorts of fast-moving possibilities.

He kept seeing Joanna Drew's face, half hidden by that scarf. Her cold eyes, the snippet of pink flesh that had been her ear. The bright blood slipping out of it . . .

If only he could feel safe again. If only he could sleep at night. If only . . . If only . . .

Reuben looked like an old man this morning, as he clambered up across Long Meadow. His face old in a way that wasn't caused by the passage of time. He seemed to be oblivious now to the wind and the rain.

He was sick of living with the fear that crawled inside him.

He had made a lot of mistakes in his life . . . his marriage the biggest one of all. 'But there won't be any more mistakes,' he grunted to himself. 'I'll see to that!'

Tom Maddocks was smiling hard, but his face was tense. His hand reached up to the pocket of his tweed jacket, dropping quickly back. His eyes touched Elizabeth's and passed swiftly on to the door. One by one, she could see him conjuring up all the usual conversation openers and rejecting them. Sometimes what people didn't say told you more than what they did.

He hadn't sounded surprised that she had asked for a meeting. Probably he had been expecting it for ages. Or a call from the police. The only thing he didn't know was where she was going to start.

She did the traditional thing and began with the weather. 'What a foul night!' She drew her jacket around her shoulders and shivered. 'It's cold up here.'

'It's always cold on the top floor in winter.' He shot a glance at her. Elizabeth smiled placidly back at him, because he had given her the perfect lead into the subject she wanted to discuss with him.

'It must cost you a fortune to heat this place?'

'You're not kidding.'

'A fortune that you haven't got,' Elizabeth said.

He laughed and attempted to throw back a flippant reply. 'My bank manager might agree with you, I fear.'

'He certainly did.'

He gazed at her, apparently searching for the joke.

Elizabeth gazed back. She could almost see his heart doing a back flip.

'You don't mean . . .? You haven't been . . .?'

'Talking to him? Of course not. But I know someone who has. Max has a friend in the local force who did some delving for us. With immensely interesting results, I might add.'

'But that's preposterous! I shall get on the phone to the bank immediately. You've no right . . . They've no right . . .'

'Bluster won't get you very far, I'm afraid, Mr Maddocks. I know about the state of your finances. I know you can't afford to pay the heating bills. Or any other bills, for that matter. So . . . I suggest we cut the crap and have a down-to-earth chat.'

She wouldn't normally have used such a crass phrase, certainly not to a born gentleman like Tom Maddocks. But if it had the advantage of shocking him into talking . . .

There was a faint noise out on the landing. A board creaking or the distant slam of a door. His eyes darted behind her. Scared, evasive eyes.

'Is there anyone else with you?'

'No, I'm on my own. For the moment.'

'I see.' He licked his lips again. Then straightened his back. He was visibly pale, but he had got over his first wave of panic.

'All right. I'll be frank with you. My father didn't leave anywhere near as much as we expected. And then there were death duties.'

'And mathematics wasn't your strong point at school. You didn't even manage a decent GCE.'

'How did you know that?'

'We checked up, Mr Maddocks. It's part of the job. I did mention that I'm a partner in Max Shepard's agency?'

'You didn't. But I heard.'

'Yes, well . . . The more I thought about it, the more the finances of this place began to intrigue me.'

There was an explosive slap of wind against the windows.

'When I first came here, I got the impression that you were a very wealthy man. Well, it was the impression that you liked to give. And you were extremely good at it, I'll grant you that. Probably came from years of practice. But then I dug under the surface a little . . .

'For example, the new computers you told Jane to get. They never actually appeared, because you cancelled the order before she signed the agreement. It was all talk. And then there's the scaffolding. It's been here for months. And when I asked my builder why he wasn't getting on with the job, I found that you'd called him off weeks ago, with some story about waiting for the better weather. But the truth is that he was getting on with the job much faster than you'd anticipated. And you simply couldn't afford to pay him. Am I right?'

A long pause. He gave the faintest of smiles.

'You're asset rich and penny poor. That's what it boils down to. You should have sold up long ago, but you just wouldn't throw in the towel . . . Neither would Joanna let you, if she could help it.'

Maddocks just stood there with a blank expression on his face.

'So you took out a second mortgage? Oh, yes, I know about that, too. You've hung on by the skin of your teeth, only surviving by moving money round and around. Robbing Peter to pay Paul . . .'

Tom Maddocks suddenly jerked his voice into life. He slammed

160

his hand down on the table in a gesture of defiance. 'It's all very well for you to make judgements. You're an outsider. But the Wetherburn's my *life*! My whole life . . .'

Elizabeth stood watching him steadily. This man who was so good at adapting his little weaknesses and getting around them so that you'd think how nice he was and how sympathetic.

The quiet of the house settled around them, broken only by the rattling of the scaffolding. Inside, her nerves were taut, but outwardly she showed nothing but cool stubbornness.

She was gazing at a man with a dodgy psyche. A man whose obsession was the bricks and mortar around him, who was besotted with the mansion and its family history. Faced with bankruptcy, what wouldn't he do to keep it?

She said, 'The other thing I found out was that Joanna had taken out a large insurance policy on her life. Now that she's dead, you'll receive thousands.'

'But I loved my sister! You're not suggesting . . .?'

Elizabeth stood quite still by the desk. Leave him. Let him talk.

'Look – to understand what Joanna means to me, you have to know what I went through here as a child.' He stopped for a moment. Swallowed hard, then started talking again so quickly that she had to listen hard to catch what he was saying. 'What both of us went through. I was a shy child. My father constantly sneered at me because I wasn't sporty. He was a bully and a despot. He tried to subdue both of us, but it only drew us closer together. Joanna wasn't as afraid of him as I was and she tried to protect me, but mostly it was no good.

'I remember one day when I broke his fishing rod. It was an accident, but it was useless to explain that when Father was in one of his moods. He beat me until the blood ran. Joanna came in after it was over. When I lay sobbing on the bed . . . She put her arms around me and tried to comfort me. She said that one day, when she was bigger, she'd kill him. She didn't, of course.'

But she might have been prepared to kill for you later in life, Elizabeth thought.

'As a young man, I was still shy and I had a slight stammer. But when he died . . . when I inherited this house, something changed in me. Looking after it and helping it survive opened me up. I found a strength that I never knew I had. I learned to go out into the world and fight for the Wetherburn. To make speeches and dream up all sorts of schemes to raise funds . . .'

'And you got married?'

'Yes.' His gaze flicked back to Elizabeth's face.

'To a woman who inherited a lot of money from her father's auctioneer's business – oh, yes, I checked up on that, too. And who proceeded to make a lot more from her books.'

'Yes.' The answer came too quickly. A barrel-load of guilt was hidden behind it.

'How much did you get Jane to invest in the Wetherburn?' There was a pause. Tom Maddocks shifted uneasily. 'How much was she demanding that you return to her, when she told you she was leaving you?'

'It wasn't like that.'

'No?'

'No.'

'I'm sorry, Mr Maddocks, but I think you're lying. I figured it out, you see. We were looking at this case from the wrong way around. We kept thinking someone was trying to kill Joanna. But I think Joanna came up here that night to murder Jane.'

'That's quite ridiculous!'

'Is it? Your sister had no intention of standing by and letting Jane bankrupt you. And Jane refused to stay in a loveless marriage, so the only solution was to kill her. She had the perfect cover in the ALF attacks. Did your sister confide in you? Did you know what she planned to do?'

'No. No, I swear it!'

'But you know now. You know what I'm talking about?'

Silence.

'So how did you find out?'

He shook his head, numbly.

'I've only got to pick up that phone, you know. Ring the police.'

'All right, all right. I . . . found her diary after she was . . . after her death.'

'Her diary? But surely the police would have found it, when they searched the cottage?'

'No. It wasn't there then.'

'So who had it?'

Another long silence. 'Quennell. Nick Quennell had it.'

162

Suddenly she understood. 'It was you who broke into his house? You were looking for the diary?'

'Yes. I knew she wrote in it every day. I knew it was missing.'

'And you had your suspicious?'

'Yes.'

'You suspected Quennell?'

'Yes. I knew someone had been at Joanna's place before the police. And there were very few people who knew where she hid the key. It had to be Quennell.'

'And when you found the diary . . .?'

'It would have incriminated her, of course.'

'She'd written it all down?'

'Yes, yes.' His face was torn with conflicting emotions. 'I can't think why . . .'

'Because she was meticulous. And she didn't expect things to go wrong, did she?'

'No. No, she didn't.' He looked weary now. 'Joanna knew that Jane was going to leave me. Well, she would have swallowed that, I suppose. They were never bosom friends and Jo would have had me all to herself once more. But she also knew I'd have had to sell up. And she knew I wouldn't have been able to bear that.'

'So she concocted an elaborate hoax?'

'Yes.'

'She invented the story of the man lurking in the lane. She even planted cigarette ends in the spot where he was supposed to have been . . . I knew there was something fishy about that.'

He looked startled. 'How?'

'Nick Quennell said that your sister recognized the man's face when he was parked in the lane. It didn't strike me until much later. The lane has a one-way system. Wherever he was parked, he'd have been facing away from her. She would have seen the back of his head, not his face. But you all fell for the story anyway. I suppose it was Joanna who fired the shots at Jane's car?'

'She hid herself behind the hedge. It was all recorded in the diary. She quite enjoyed playing scared and fooling everybody.'

'She even went so far as to have extra locks fitted on her doors . . . And bought the rape alarm. Your sister was a clever lady.'

'Cleverer than me. Always was.'

163

'And so, when she'd done enough groundwork and set the scene, she walked up to the Wetherburn with the gun in her pocket?'

'Yes. She planned to wait until I was away for the night. So that no one could incriminate me, if it all went wrong.'

Which it did, Elizabeth thought grimly.

'She took the ALF leaflet to drop by the body . . . And she walked up across the field with the dogs . . .'

'That's why they were locked into the old pantry,' Elizabeth said. 'She didn't want them making a noise . . .' She thought about Anderson's meeting. Thanks, Persephone.

'She'd dithered about taking them at all, but she finally decided that they were good cover if anyone happened to see her going up there.'

'But her plans went awry . . .'

'It seems so.'

The silence in the room was visibly disconcerting. She let it go on and on. Then Tom Maddocks turned his head and looked her in the eyes.

'I killed Joanna, Mrs Blair,' he said.

She was startled. 'You came back that night, unexpectedly?'

'I wish to God I had!' White-knuckled, his hand gripped the chairback. 'What I meant was that if I'd been at home instead of out touting for funds for the Wetherburn, it might never have happened.' There was no self-pity in the tersely uttered words. Just bleakness. 'What will I do with my life without Joanna? We've always carried the weight of this place between us.'

Suddenly, he shot out a hand to grip her arm. 'What are you going to do? You can't tell the police.'

'I can't tell anyone until I hear the rest of the story. Your sister had locked the dogs in the pantry . . .'

Tom said, dully, 'Your guess is as good as mine. The diary stopped. And I wasn't here the night she died, was I?'

'Max? It's Elizabeth.'

'Elizabeth . . . I can't talk to you now.'

'You have to. I want you to meet me in Nick Quennell's office at the Wetherburn. First floor back. I'll leave the door undone. Say seven thirty?'

'I told you. I can't.'

'Max? You sound odd. What's wrong?'

'It's Helen. She's gone. She's taken the kids and run. She's gone to Ireland to be with her parents. I've got to go after her.'

'Is that wise? Listen – take time to think.'

'I can't. I can't just leave it.'

'Believe me, Max, it might be better.'

'But I love her. And she wanted to be with me. I know she did.'

'Max . . . we'll talk about it later. It's imperative that you get your mind back on the Wetherburn job. Listen, I had a letter, too. Want me to read it out to you?'

Damn it, he'd put the phone down. Now she wouldn't know whether he'd be there or not. She gazed at the piece of paper that was spread out on her desk. But she had to go anyway. Time was running out . . .

24

Nick Quennell seemed to Elizabeth to be uneasy. He wouldn't take a seat, but preferred to stand by the cold of the window. (The draught was moving the long curtain and lifting it inwards an inch or two.) He said offhandedly to Elizabeth, 'It's very late. I don't know what's so important that can't wait until tomorrow.'

It had been a spur of the moment decision, summoning him up here. Elizabeth had not wanted to meet in his cottage. There was something about the physical presence of the Wetherburn, its airless rooms and its corridors and tall, rectangular proportions, that was almost threatening.

'I thought you might prefer to talk where your wife can't hear,' Elizabeth said. Quennell looked apprehensive. She gave him time to reflect on this. To let it sink right in, where it would do most damage.

'What's this about?' he asked.

She said bluntly, 'I'd like to know where you were on the night Joanna Drew was murdered.'

'We're back to that again?'

'We're back to that again.'

He decided to humour her. 'I told you . . . Lucy had a bad day and the doctor gave her something to make her sleep. I took the phone off the hook and settled down to some work in my study.'

'The doctor gave her something? Are you sure it wasn't one of Ted Anderson's quack medicines?'

He flushed. There was a new edge to his voice as he said, 'Presumably you've been listening to my son. Well, you've got the wrong end of the stick. Anderson's herbal stuff is quite harmless and Lucy believes in it, otherwise I wouldn't waste my money on it.'

There was a little pause. 'So . . . you didn't see anything that night?'

'Nothing.'

'You were working all evening?'

'Yes. I told you.'

'You have no idea what time Mrs Drew went out with her dogs?'

'Look – I didn't see anything. I didn't hear anything. Why don't you believe me?'

'Mr Quennell, do you know where Mrs Drew hid her front door key when she went out?'

'I haven't a clue. Why should I?'

'I just thought you might, that's all.'

'Well, you thought wrong.'

'Only your cleaning lady . . . Mrs Watts . . . knows. She fishes it out from under a stone by the porch when she goes from your place to Mrs Drew's on a Friday.'

'Well, I didn't know! Christ, why should I, with all that I've got on my plate?'

'So you didn't tell Mrs Watts where to find it when she first came down here to work?'

He changed colour at that. 'No . . . I don't think so. Joanna must have told her.'

'I should tell you that I've spoken to Mrs Watts.'

'What if you have? The woman's not too bright.'

'Bright enough to testify in court, Mr Quennell.'

His expression changed, but he made no reply.

Elizabeth said, 'OK. We'll move on. Tell me about Joanna Drew's diary.'

He just stood there.

She watched the heart attack he very nearly had.

He looked down at the rug. Now his colour had gone altogether, he was dead white.

'Mr Quennell?'

He said, 'How did you find out?'

'Tom Maddocks. He was your intruder.'

'So he read it all? He knows . . .'

Steady, Elizabeth thought. Don't take your eyes off his. Let him assume that you agree. 'You were up here that night . . . You surprised Joanna.'

For a moment, he hesitated, then he caved in. 'All right. Yes, I was here that night. I knew Tom was away and I wanted to see Jane so much.'

'So the affair wasn't over?'

'No. I lied to you about that. I sat there in my study until I couldn't stand it any longer . . . The doctor had given Lucy something to make her sleep. She was out for the count. Tim had gone out clubbing. In the end, I locked the door behind me and I slipped up across the field.'

'Just like Joanna.'

'Just like Joanna.'

'You took a torch?'

'Yes. There was a moon, but it kept going behind the clouds.'

'What time was this?'

'I'm not sure. Eight fifteen-ish. Somewhere around then.'

'Did you ring Jane?'

'No. She wasn't expecting me. She didn't even know I was there until . . . until Joanna . . .' In a low voice, he said, 'I'd got to the end of the house. As I came round the side of the terrace, I saw that the lights were on in the Exhibition Centre. She's working, I thought. She's up there working on the exhibition.'

'Jane?'

'Yes.'

'On her own? At night?'

'They were desperately behind. She had no choice, she told me later. Anyway, the Exhibition Centre wasn't far from the house. Across the drive and up a few steps. She was up there working and . . . and just as I was about to cross the drive, I saw Joanna.

She came out of the shadows and she actually had a gun in her hand.'

'You saw that in the dark?'

'Not at first. But then she crossed into the patch of light from the open door.'

'Why was the door open? It was a cold night.'

'I don't know. It just was. Maybe Jane had left it ajar and the wind took it. At first, I couldn't move. You hear people say they're rooted to the spot. Well, that's exactly how it is. God knows how long it was before I realized that she was actually going to use the gun. When she got inside the door, I suppose, and said something to Jane. Her voice sounded so odd.'

'What did she say?'

'That's the strange thing. I couldn't tell you. All I know is that she sounded cold and harsh and I knew, quite suddenly, what she was going to do. That's when I started to run.' Nick looked up, straight into Elizabeth's eyes. 'I didn't know I could move so fast. I knocked her into the room as I went for her. And the gun must have gone off as she went down. She was stronger than I imagined. The gun went off twice more as we struggled. Jane was screaming . . . It seemed to go on for ever . . . At last I got the gun away from her, but she gave one last lunge at me and it went off and she fell. She would have killed me as well, you know,' he said with a kind of fascinated horror. 'She was as mad as hell that I arrived to stop her.'

He paused, as if to gether himself together, but he still hadn't finished.

'And then, of course, we had to decide what to do. The place was a shambles and I had blood all over my shirt. We closed the door on it and we got ourselves back to the flat somehow or other. I poured a couple of stiff brandies and later – much later – it came to us that Joanna had set up the perfect cover for us, providing we kept our heads. She'd told Margaret Fleming that she was worried about Jane, so all we had to do was say that Joanna had walked up there to check and had surprised an ALF intruder. She'd laid all the false clues . . . everything. All we had to do was keep our heads.

'We tried to think of everything. We removed the gun and I kicked in the door lock, so that it would look as if the intruder had broken in. I sprinkled petrol around – just a bit – and left the can there. The ALF leaflet had fallen out of Joanna's pocket in the struggle . . .'

'And the Indian scarf?'

'That was Jane's idea – to make it look like a case of mistaken identity. We draped it around Joanna's head. And then, when I'd calmed Jane down, I went home and changed out of my blood-stained clothes . . . and shoes . . . and I bundled them up with the gun and hid them behind lumber in the shed until I could dispose of them.'

'Where?'

'Where? In the canal. And then, when she'd given me enough time to do all that, Jane rang the police. Her hysteria on the phone was the real thing.'

'It must have been pretty difficult for her to face her husband. Tell me, how did she know he wasn't in on Joanna's little scheme?'

'She didn't. That was the most difficult thing of all. She had to stay there and watch and listen and just hope that he wasn't. Because if Tom was in on it, then he might have another go at getting rid of her.'

'But she couldn't cut and run, because it would have looked suspicious?'

'Exactly.'

Elizabeth sat there thinking. So many people laying false trails, both physical and emotional. You needed time to take it all in.

'And Laura Eyton?' she said quietly.

'Laura? It's quite simple. Laura snooped around too much. She happened to be in the stationery cupboard when I was talking to Jane in the corridor. She overheard something and put two and two together and she summoned me to the shop late one night and she told me she was going to the police.' For the first time, he looked almost relieved to get it off his chest, as though he could talk now without any restrictions. 'I couldn't let her do that, of course. For Jane's sake. For Lucy's sake. How would she go on if I got a prison sentence? There'd be nobody to look after her. I wasn't having her put into an institution.'

'So you killed Laura?'

'Yes.' He admitted it almost with relief. 'I don't think I intended to at first. But she started laughing and I lost my temper. I'd gone

169

through so much in the last couple of years and she was laughing at me. I saw red. I hit her and then, somehow, my hands were round her throat . . .'

'And this time, when you threw the petrol around, you set it alight?'

'It seemed the best way to destroy any evidence.'

'Did Jane know about this?'

'Not until afterwards. I didn't tell her I was going to see Laura. She had enough to worry about and I was afraid she might snap.'

'But she didn't? I'm assuming you told her after the fire?'

'I had to.'

'And?'

'And she was horrified, of course. But once you get in deep . . .'

You keep digging yourself in deeper, Elizabeth thought. She was filled with a strange mixture of misgiving and curiosity. 'So how much of all this have you told your son?'

'Nothing. Nothing at all.' He put his hands in his jacket pockets. His lips had tightened.

Elizabeth got up and walked to the window. There was a plank walk outside and a geometric tangle of scaffolding half lit by the light from the office. He's going to have a breakdown, she thought. Some time soon – I wonder when? She stood and gazed, at black metal and nuts and bolts, a little longer. Then she turned abruptly and threw the spanner in the works.

'There's just one thing I'd like to clear up.'

'What's that?'

'You say you were alone up here with Jane?'

'Yes.'

'No one else at all came all evening?'

'No. I told you.'

'Then what,' she said, drawing the folded envelope from her pocket, 'did Ruth Dando mean when she sent me this?'

His eyes, myopic behind the gold-rimmed spectacles, gazed at the envelope. 'Ruth Dando?'

'Yes. She posted a letter to me yesterday, before she left her husband. It has some interesting information in it.'

He shrugged. 'What's it got to do with me?'

Elizabeth said steadily, 'Quite a lot, as it happens. The letter says

170

that Reuben had a phone call from Jane at around eight forty-five on the night Joanna was murdered. That he came rushing up here immediately after.'

'I . . . that's ridiculous! I've told you what happened. Reuben didn't come near the place. She must have got it wrong. She's always been jealous of her husband's friendship with Jane. The woman's obsessed. She must have been mistaken . . .'

'You think so?'

'I'm sure of it.'

'Well, we'll see.'

'What does that mean?'

'It means that I've asked a few other people to pop up here. If you're right, Jane will be able to confirm your story. So we'll just stay hunkered down here until she arrives, if that's all right with you?'

25

Elizabeth sat watching them all. The heavy bookshelves all round the room made an uncompromisingly dark backcloth to the drama that was about to unfold. There were barely enough chairs, but Reuben Dando had planted his solid frame on to a not-so-solid side table. It creaked every time he moved and Elizabeth expected one of its flimsy legs to snap at any minute.

'Nick? What are you doing here?' Jane Maddocks had asked, quite thrown by his presence. 'I thought Mrs Blair and I were going to talk quilts.'

She was wearing a long, dark skirt and a bright Indian waistcoat, embroidered in fine gold and pink threads, very ethnic, very exotic. And she had tied her hair up in a thin, gold scarf. She looked small and vibrant and more like an appealing girl than the mother of a grown-up daughter.

Tom Maddocks, on the other hand, looked as if he had aged ten years. He had greeted Elizabeth with elaborate uneasiness and sat now by the door with his hands on his knees. Elizabeth watched him out of the corner of her eye and reflected that, however much he had told her the other night, he probably knew more – a lot more than he was letting on.

'Nick – what's this about?' Jane asked again. 'Is something wrong? Who's sitting with Lucy?'

'The nurse,' Quennell said. When he looked at her, the brooding in his eyes changed to alertness.

The alarm tinkled on Elizabeth's watch. A quarter before eight. Where the hell was Max? She needed him. But she was surprised how calm her voice sounded.

'I sent you all a note asking you to meet me here because I'm curious. And persistent. And I'm sick of being fed lies about the death of Joanna Drew.'

There was no sound now in the room. She noticed that Reuben was edging his bulk away from the table. She also noticed that Tom was sweating, on his forehead and temples. After a moment's thought, she turned to Jane.

'First, I'd like to know who was up here that night.'

'No one. Just me.'

'I really wanted the truth.'

'That is the truth.' There was just the faintest hint of aggression in her voice. She sat staring down at her black-clad legs.

'OK.' Elizabeth turned her attention to Reuben. 'You know, I was thinking, it's a funny thing that Joanna Drew was killed on the only night of the week you weren't patrolling the grounds, Mr Dando. Quite a coincidence, in fact.'

As she spoke, she slowly drew the sheet of notepaper from her pocket. She watched his reaction as he recognized his wife's hand-writing on it.

He knew when the game was up. 'All right,' he said. 'I'll admit it. I killed Joanna.'

There was a fractional pause and then Elizabeth said, 'Great heavens! Are there any more offers, while we're at it?'

'Don't you believe me?' He stood there glowering at her.

Elizabeth hadn't quite put the whole jigsaw together, but she had enough of the picture to doubt Reuben's claim. 'Well,' she said, 'I do believe you were up here that night, but I rather think you'd have shaken Mrs Drew like a rat. Shooting was too good for her, don't you think?'

Tom was looking at her. He looked white with fury.

'I killed her, I tell you! She . . . she went for Jane –'

'Yes, well, the only trouble is, I've heard that one before. It's stale news.'

'Oh, for God's sake! You bloody fool!' Quennell was on his feet now.

'Fool, am I? Well, who started blabbing first?' Reuben advanced towards him, breathing heavily, his clenched fists like sledge-hammers.

'Stop it! Stop it, both of you!'

Jane was on her feet, too. The expression on her face was all but indescribable. Guilty yet angry. Stricken yet fearful. The long window gave a sharp rattle as the wind hit it.

She said, almost in a whisper, 'It's no use. I've had enough. I'm too tired to go on with this charade . . .'

Elizabeth said, 'It was you who really killed her.'

'Yes, yes, yes,' Jane said. Elizabeth had never seen anyone cave in quite so fast. 'She tried to kill me. I had to defend myself.'

Minutes later, gripping her head with both hands, she told the full story. 'I was in the Exhibition Centre, putting the circus procession in place. I was really absorbed, working away. And then I felt a blast of cold air. I looked around – and there was Joanna standing in the doorway. I thought, Oh, God, not now. I was so busy, you see. I didn't want to stop and talk. Particularly to Joanna. She goes on and on about such trivial things and you can't get rid of her. Sorry, unfortunate choice of words. And it should all be in the past tense . . . but it feels as if she's still here, dominating us all.'

Tom's face was a mask. All expression erased by inner emptiness.

'I said something like, "There's really no need." You see, she'd been fussing on so much about this man in the lane. Acting all kind and caring. Not at all her usual style.' She caught Tom's expression. 'I'm sorry, but it wasn't. You know how she treated me in private. Patronizing and scornful. She brushed me off, as if I didn't really belong here. As if I wasn't good enough for her precious Wether-burn – which was rich, considering how much I'd put into it. Anyway, she didn't reply. And I thought that was odd, because she was never short of an answer. She just kept walking towards me with this staring look in her eyes. So I said again, "Look – you needn't fuss. I'm perfectly safe." And she said, "Are you?" Which, again, was an odd thing to say.'

The windows rattled again as the wind gusted.

' "You might be wrong about that," Joanna said and I still didn't have a clue what she was talking about. "Did you see something?" I asked her. "What on earth is it?" And she said something even more peculiar. "I've had this fight with my conscience, but I silenced it in the end. Morals don't really count, you see, in the real world. Not if you love someone enough." And then she drew her hand out of her pocket and I saw the gun. I still didn't believe she was going to use it. I thought, she's flipped her lid. I mean, I'd heard about the new locks and the rape alarm. I thought, this is her latest weapon against the ALF. How ludicrous. But then she lifted it and pointed it at me . . . and I thought, It's me she's aiming at . . . Good God, is this a joke? But Joanna never had a sense of humour and a split second later, I thought, She means it. She's actually going to kill me.

' "I can't let you destroy him," that's what Joanna said quite calmly, before she pulled the trigger. "He should never have married you." She wasn't much of a shot. That was what saved me. I leapt sideways and she wasn't expecting that. She missed with the second shot, too, and that's when the wrestling match started. I had to get the gun off her. We finished up on the floor. I thanked God that I was younger and fitter, but she still fought like a tigress. I managed to wrench the gun away, but she still kept coming. It went off . . . caught her ear. Still she came back at me . . . it was like a nightmare . . . the blood, the names she spat at me . . . She just wouldn't give in. The last shot . . . it was an accident. She just dropped and that was the end . . .

'I didn't know what to do. I was in shock. I sat there on the floor for what seemed like hours. And then I got myself back to the house and I tried to ring Nick. But he'd disconnected the phone.'

'And that's when you rang Reuben?'

'I couldn't think of anyone else.'

Reuben said, 'When I got there, she was walking around in a daze. Still in shock. "I mustn't panic," she kept saying. "Mustn't panic. Mustn't panic . . ." And she was shaking like a leaf, so I sat her down and gave her some brandy. And persuaded her to change out of her bloodstained clothes.'

Elizabeth said, 'You didn't think of ringing the police? Pleading self-defence?'

'I couldn't. I was too frightened. And then Nick arrived . . . I don't know how much later . . . and we had to decide what we were going to do. It was Nick's idea to continue the myth of the ALF intruder . . . Once we'd decided on that, Nick hared down to Joanna's cottage to check that there was nothing there that would reveal her plans to the police. That's when he removed the diary. If the police had found it, they'd have known I had to be involved.' She was no longer looking at Elizabeth, but at Tom. 'Did you know about her plans?'

'No.' He said to Quennell, 'I'd have sacked you months ago if it weren't for Lucy's illness. It'll kill her to see you in court. You realize that?'

'How can you say such a thing?' There was vitriol now in her eyes as she advanced towards him. 'But then, you always did know how to put the knife in. If anyone goes to jail, it should be you. All our married life, this place had to come first. It's already cost two lives. For God's sake, how many more have to be sacrificed to your bloody obsession?'

He gazed back at her. 'Oh, I don't think that argument will cut much ice with the police.'

Reuben turned on him. 'You bastard!'

'Of course,' Tom said, never letting his smile slip for a moment, 'I'll plead with them for leniency. Make as good a show as I can, but the details of her relationships with all her fancy men won't look good in the press.'

Reuben's face was brick-red. He said, 'Shut your mouth. If you'd been a decent husband to her –'

Tom actually laughed. 'Isn't that a case of the pot calling the kettle? I understand your wife flew the coop yesterday. Cleared off to Germany to live with her sister. Well, I should think that's far enough away from your foul temper.'

Reuben lunged forward. He slammed Tom Maddocks against the bookcase.

'Shut your mouth, or I'll shut it for you!'

'Ever hit Ruth, did you? I once heard –'

'Jane –'

Nick Quennell moved between her and Elizabeth.

'Get out of here. Now!'

She threw him a stunned look, then ran for the door.

Reuben hadn't heard anything that had been said. He was propelling Tom Maddocks away from the cupboard and was slamming his fist into his stomach. Tom crashed moaning to the floor. Reuben slammed a foot hard into his grey-flannelled backside.

Elizabeth wished Max was there. She didn't know whether to head for Reuben or Jane Maddocks, who, after an agonized glance back at Nick, had gone out of the door.

She decided on Jane. (Reuben had now noticed her absence and was standing there getting his breath back together.) 'Get out of my way!' she said to Nick, who was gripping her by the arms to make sure that Jane had a good, long start.

'Not . . . yet.' Nick's voice shook.

Elizabeth struggled to free herself. 'You're not helping her.'

'I'll be the judge of that.'

Reuben said to Nick, 'My car's outside. I'll look after her. They won't find her.'

'She won't want you. She'll take her own car.'

'But you can't let her go like that.'

'She's better off on her own. You'll draw attention to her.'

'How the hell would I do that?'

'Listen – she won't want you! She's sick of you fussing round her . . .'

God, Elizabeth thought, they're fighting over her like two schoolkids. In a minute, they'll be calling each other names. Yah boo, sucks to you. And with Tom lying on the floor groaning. It was perfectly ridiculous.

Abruptly, she kneed Quennell where it hurt most.

'Oomph!' He doubled up in pain and as soon as his grip loosened, she made for the door. She heard Reuben yell as she shot out into the passage. He came after her, but he couldn't move as fast as she could. She hit the main staircase at breakneck speed (well, for her) and didn't stop until she was down in the hall.

The front door seemed to have stuck. It was swollen with the damp and Jane had slammed it hard as she went.

At last, however, Elizabeth wrenched it open. And the outer door in the porch.

The drive turned sharply by the terrace steps. Car lights, coming from the direction of the village, came sweeping round the bend. Jane paused briefly, as if uncertain, made a dash for her own car, which was parked on the far side of the sweep of gravel. Max had no warning. She shot out just as he would have got his first glimpse of the house. He braked as hard as he could, of course, but there was no avoiding her. She hit the top of his bonnet and landed on the holly bank on the far side.

She had no memory, later, of the accident. She was unconscious for weeks.

26

Thanksgiving. Elizabeth was carving the turkey. For some reason, she didn't fancy it as much as other years. But there was always the mince pie, the pumpkin pie and the sweet potato.

The table was spread in front of the window. Max had come over. (Well, the boy had to eat and they couldn't have him moping over there on his own.) There was enough food to last them for a month.

'So Joanna was forcing Oliver to cook the books because of Tom's financial problems, not her own?' Max said.

'That's right.'

There was a pause. 'Did Jane really have an affair with Reuben, as well as Nick?'

'Shouldn't think so for one minute. She needed to talk over her problems with an old friend. And Reuben had always been there for her.'

'The other thing that's puzzling me is who doused Reuben's car with paint that night.'

'That's easy. Reuben did it himself to keep the ALF myth going. Anything to divert suspicion from Jane.'

'Expensive gesture,' Hal said.

'He was desperately in love. Still is.'

'After all those years . . . Sad,' Hal said.

'Oh, I don't know. Some folks would give their eye teeth to feel that kind of passion.'

'Even though it's unreciprocated?' Max stood there looking at her.

'Even then. Love's never wasted, Max.'

She distributed the plates and took the chair at the end of the table. 'Say grace, Hal.'

Max looked uneasy.

'Can't have Thanksgiving dinner without grace.'

'We thank Thee, O Lord, for our food. And the love that's around this table.'

'Amen. Dig in, folks.'

They ate for a while. Then Max said, 'What about Lucy? What's happening to her?'

'Tim's at home.'

'Yes, but what a burden.'

'Philly's going to help.'

'What about his college course?'

'Deferred for a while.'

'And the Wetherburn?'

'Tom's still fighting to keep it open. Depends if he gets Joanna's insurance money, I suppose. Which is perhaps debatable, seeing that his wife killed her.'

'But Joanna may still get her way in the end?'

'I guess.'

'Sometimes,' Max said, 'you feel the wrong people win.' He reached glumly for his glass. 'And lose.'

'You're no loser, Max.'

'No?'

She gazed across at him. She said firmly, so firmly that he would have to take heed for once in his life, 'You'd better believe it.'